Like a Flower in the Field

C.W. SPOONER

LIKE A FLOWER IN THE FIELD

iUniverse books may be ordered through booksellers or by contacting:

iUniverse
1663 Liberty Drive
Bloomington, IN 47403
www.iuniverse.com
1-800-Authors (1-800-288-4677)

ISBN: 978-1-5320-2297-5 (sc)
ISBN: 978-1-5320-2298-2 (e)

Library of Congress Control Number: 2017906786

Print information available on the last page.

iUniverse rev. date: 05/02/2017

For my grandchildren…
Elyssia, Travis, Cole, Logan
Mason, Collin, Kamille
Samantha, Emily, and River
…and great grandchildren…
Robyn, Dylan, Malena, and Charlie
…with love.

Also by the author:

'68 – A Novel
Children of Vallejo – Collected Stories of a Lifetime
Yeah, What Else? – Essays, Memoirs, Poems, and Reviews

CONTENTS

PREFACE

There are places in your life that leave an indelible mark. It might be the town where you grew up, or where you settled to raise your family, or maybe it's the locale you chose for Act Three—caring for grandchildren, watching them grow.

The question is: do we leave a mark on the places we've been? When we're gone, will anything remain? There's a verse from Psalm 103 that speaks to these questions:

> Man, his days are those of grass
> He flourishes like a flower in the field
> A wind passes by and it is no more
> Its own place no longer knows it.

The stories in this collection are from the places in my life. I've divided them into four sections: The Dock of the Bay; The Big Tomato; Other Places – Other Lives; and Three Hundred Sunny Days. No need to explain. You'll know the place when you get there.

Most tales begin with a kernel of truth, some event—large or small—to build a yarn around. The kernels that make me want to sit at the keyboard and hammer out a story are coming to mind less frequently.

I'd better hurry, before a wind passes by.

-C.W.S.
March 2017

THE DOCK OF THE BAY

"It was a serious journey, traveling from Vallejo
to San Francisco in those days…
This was the era (early 1950s) before
Interstate 80 and the "big cut,"
when U.S. 40 crossed the Carquinez
Bridge and swung to the west,
following the shoreline through all the
towns that rimmed the bay:
Crockett, Rodeo, Hercules, Pinole, San
Pablo, Richmond, Albany, Berkeley,
and finally Emeryville and the majestic
Bay Bridge into The City."

-C.W.S. from *Yeah, What Else?*

"San Francisco is the only city I can think of
that can survive all the things you people are doing to it
and still look beautiful."

-Frank Lloyd Wright

CHASIN' THE BIRD

from *Monday Update*

D ominic buried his face in the pillow, hanging on to the last vestiges of a good night's sleep. He had a rare Monday off, a "use it or lose it" vacation day. Della came into the room and sat down on the bed. She leaned down to kiss him on the temple and he had to smile. There she was, showered and dressed, makeup expertly applied, her dark curly hair framing her face. God she was cute. Dom was wide awake now.

"Okay, baby, I'm off to work." She fiddled with an earring, adjusting the clasp.

"You sure you have to go? You smell so good I could eat you up."

"Hmmm, hold that thought. I've got meetings scheduled this morning. I'm going to be late as is. What are your plans for the day?"

Dom rolled over and clasped his hands behind his head. "I'm going over to Vinnie's place, see if he needs anything."

"Okay. Tell him I said 'Hi.' You know, we should have him over for dinner. He hasn't been here for a while."

"Yeah, but you know how he is. He's got his routine. Goes to work, comes home, has something to eat, listens to his jazz, and goes to sleep. He doesn't like change."

"You know, Dom, I don't think your brother likes me. I think that's part of it."

"Nah, he's just shy, especially around pretty girls." He squeezed her knee and she jumped a little.

"Stop it. I'm serious. I don't think Vinnie likes me."

Dom started to protest, but he could see the concern on Della's face. "I'll talk to him today. If there's a problem we'll work it out. You know Vinnie—he's an open book. And I'll invite him for dinner. Okay?"

"Okay. Let's do it Friday night. I'll make lasagna. Oh, I gotta go. Give Vinnie my love."

She was off the bed and headed for the door before Dom could grab her and convince her to stay. There was nobody like Della, at least no one Dom had ever met. Smart, feisty, funny, ambitious. He'd already made up his mind to put a ring on that finger, and soon, before she could discover all of his faults.

He checked the clock on the bedside table. Only 7:35. He'd told Vinnie to expect him by 10:00 and it was just a short drive from Dom's apartment near the Panhandle of Golden Gate Park; plenty of time to shower and shave and make a plan for the day. Vinnie loved it when Dom came with a plan.

Vincent Thomas Mancini was thirty-nine on his last birthday, three years older than Dom. Vinnie had intellectual disabilities. The doctors said he was "somewhere on the spectrum," that long arc of autism and other developmental issues that continues to evolve. He lived independently in a rented room in San Francisco, just a block or two from the cable car barn. He had the upper floor of a home owned by a widow, Dorothy Kemper, who kept an eye on him, packed a lunch for him to take to work, and put a hot meal on the table most evenings. Vinnie worked four days a week in the mail room of an office down on Market Street, and he took great pride in his job. It gave him a little spending money and, even more important, a sense of independence. Their parents had left an estate large enough to provide everything that Vinnie needed—room and board, clothes, medical insurance—all the necessities of life, including the means to continue building his collection of classic jazz CD's. No iPod or downloads for Vinnie. He liked to hold a jewel case in his hands, with its colorful cover art and liner notes tucked inside.

Dom bounced out of bed and headed for the bathroom. Being late for Vinnie was not an option.

———⁓ᴡ°ᴏᴏⱻᴏⴳⱻᴏᴏᴡᴡ———

Vinnie opened the door as Dom was walking up the marble steps to Mrs. Kemper's place.

"Hey, Dominic, what's up? Ten o'clock, right on time." He gave Dom a bear hug, lifting him off the floor.

"Ow, Vinnie, you're gonna break a rib." They laughed as Vinnie put him down. "Hey, I brought something for you. Wanna see it?"

"For me? Oh yeah, let's see." He was excited now. Vinnie loved presents.

Dom handed him a CD that he'd found online: *The Cal Tjader Sextet – A Night at the Black Hawk.*

"Oh, man! Thanks, Dom. I don't have this one. I'm going to listen to it tonight. This is great."

Seeing Vinnie smiling, excited, and happy gave Dom a good feeling. They'd both inherited their mother's curly red hair and when they were younger, people often mistook them for twins. Mom was in her forties, their father in his fifties, when the boys were born. Heart disease had claimed both parents when the boys were in their mid-twenties.

"So, Vinnie, I figure we'll make a list and go to the Safeway down in the Marina. And if you need anything, you know, clothes or socks or underwear, we can go downtown to Macy's. And we'll get some lunch while we're out. How's that sound?"

Vinnie was busy reading the back of the CD. "What? Oh yeah, Dom, that's great. Let me put this away and I'll grab my jacket."

He trotted up the stairs to his room leaving Dom in the

entryway. This home was perfect for Vinnie, just a block from the cable car line. He could ride that venerable antique everywhere he needed to go—downtown for work or shopping around Union Square, down to Aquatic Park to enjoy the waterfront, or over to Fisherman's Wharf for seafood, and then back home to Mrs. Kemper's. As Della would say, it was "very San Francisco."

Vinnie came down the stairs, his jacket partly off one shoulder. Dom helped him straighten it and zip it to the collar. It was August and a cold wind was whipping through the streets of the neighborhood. If you wanted summer in San Francisco, you had to wait for September and October.

———⚬⚬⚬⚬⚬———

The brothers smiled across the table at the Washington Square Bar & Grill—the Washbag as Herb Caen dubbed it—the fabled restaurant at the corner of Powell and Union. Vinnie loved the filet of sole with lemon-butter-caper sauce. They both ordered the sole, plus a 7-Up for Vinnie and a glass of Chardonnay for Dom.

"So, Vinnie, how was your week?" Dom knew what the answer would be, a variation on the same old theme.

"Oh it was great, Dom. I caught Miles Davis at the Black Hawk. Turk and Hyde, 'The Jazz Corner of the West.' What a dump!" He laughed out loud. "Two sets, both of 'em great. Miles is the best..."

There was a time when Dom would have tried to correct his brother, to explain patiently that the Black Hawk closed decades ago and Miles was dead and gone. What Vinnie had done was sit for hours in his room, his headphones in place, listening to *Miles Davis – In Person at the Black Hawk*, a classic recorded in 1961. But Dom had given up on corrections. If Vinnie believed he was there, hearing Miles in the flesh, so be it.

"So, it was a great show. How was the crowd?"

"Out the door and around the block, man. SRO! But listen,

Dom, the best thing all week was Bird. Bird is here in San Francisco! I heard him, man, several times."

Dom was sure Vinnie was referring to another CD, one of many Charlie "Bird" Parker recordings that he owned. "Oh really? Where is he playing?"

"He's all over, man. I heard him up in Union Square, then over by Macy's, and then down by the Buena Vista. Playing all his classics, 'Star Eyes' and 'Confirmation' and 'Yardbird Suite.' Never better, Dom. You've never heard 'Star Eyes' so beautiful. You gotta come with me. We should go find him—"

"Yeah, Vinnie. But not today. Maybe another time. Okay?" Dom paused a moment. "Hey, Della wants you to come over for dinner on Friday. How's that sound?"

Vinnie looked away. "Yeah, okay, dinner on Friday."

"Vinnie, what's wrong? Is there a problem?"

"No, Dom. No problem."

"Vinnie, look at me. Let me see your eyes." Dom waited until his brother turned toward him. "Della is afraid you don't like her. Tell me the truth, Vinnie. Are you okay with Della?"

"Yeah, she's great, Dom. It's just, well you know..."

"Come on, Vinnie, tell me."

"We don't do things together...like we used to."

"Is that it? I don't spend as much time with you as before?"

"Yeah, I guess." Vinnie looked away again.

"Vin, look at me." Dom waited. "Hey, you're my big brother and I love you. We'll work this out. All right? We'll work on it. I promise I'll do better."

It wasn't long until Dom had Vinnie smiling again, back to his tale of Charlie Parker alive and well, playing on the streets of the city they loved. Dom was relieved, and he knew Della would be too.

5

Dominic unlocked the door, Vinnie close behind him, stuck his head in and called, "Hey Lucy, I'm home."

Della's voice rang out from the kitchen: "Ricky you're so fine, you're so fine you blow my mind…Hey Ricky, Hey Ricky."

It was their riff on the Weird Al Yankovic parody, always good for a laugh. Della came out to greet them, a smudged white apron tied around her waist.

"Hi, Vinnie!" She gave him a quick hug and a kiss on the cheek. He flinched a little. "I hope you're hungry. I'm making lasagna, from your mom's recipe."

"Oh hi, Della. Yeah, Mom's lasagna, thanks for having me over." Vinnie avoided eye contact. Then he remembered the bouquet of flowers in his hand, purchased with his hard-earned money from a stand on Powell Street. "Oh, these are for you, Della." He held them out proudly.

"Oh, thank you, Vinnie. How sweet!" She started to kiss him again but hesitated. "I'll put these in a vase." She hurried away to the kitchen.

Dom took his brother's jacket and flashed a thumbs-up. Vinnie smiled. This was a good beginning.

The dinner conversation followed the usual pattern, each party recounting the events of the week just ended. When it was Vinnie's turn, they were not surprised—at least not at first.

"I saw the Cannonball Adderley Quintet, live at The Jazz Workshop. It was great. What a crowd. You could barely get in the place. They played Bobby Timmons's 'This Here.' Great tune, man. It's gonna be a hit. Guaranteed."

Vinnie went on to describe the entire performance, which Dom had heard before. The live recording from 1959 was one of Vinnie's favorites. With barely a pause, he segued into his next story and his enthusiasm cranked up a notch.

"…and Bird is still here, Dom. He's still in San Francisco, playing all over town. You've got to come with me, Bro. You'll love it. All the classics, 'Moose the Mooche,' 'Scrapple from the Apple,' 'Ko Ko.' And you've never heard 'Star Eyes' played like this—"

"Vinnie, wait a second. Are you saying there's a guy playing on the street that sounds like Charlie Parker? Is that it?"

"Yeah, man, it's Bird, here in The City by the Golden Gate, Baghdad by the Bay, don't call it Frisco—"

"Okay, okay, calm down. I promise we'll go real soon. All right? We'll chase down the Bird."

The conversation moved on to other topics. Vinnie loved the lasagna, and the bouquet of flowers was lovely in the little vase. Dom would count this evening a success.

———~~∘⊙⚬⊛⊙⚬∘~~———

"Hey Lucy, I'm home." Dom came through the front door with the usual greeting.

Della came out of the kitchen quickly, holding the cordless phone toward him. "It's the police," she said, her face drained of color.

Dom took the phone from her. "Hello."

"Mr. Mancini, this is Sergeant Donlan, San Francisco Police. Sir, your brother was stabbed in an altercation in Union Square. He had a card in his wallet listing you as an emergency contact. He's been taken to San Francisco General, the trauma center."

"Oh my God! What happened?"

"He was listening to a street musician and three young males came along and started grabbing money out of the man's instrument case. Your brother charged them and threw a body block that knocked two of them down. The third one stabbed your brother with a switchblade. The three of them ran off."

"How is..." Dom choked on his words. "Is Vinnie okay?"

"I can't answer that, Mr. Mancini. I suggest you get to the hospital as soon as you can."

Della grabbed her coat and purse. They locked the front door and ran for Dom's car. Fog crept over the hills, about to engulf the neighborhood as they sped toward S.F. General.

The trauma center waiting room was a busy place, people coming and going, families huddled together, speaking in hushed tones. Periodically a doctor would appear through the wide automatic doors, find the appropriate family members and give them a brief status report. The reactions ran the gamut, from smiles and laughter and hugs for the doctor, to choked sobs and tears.

Dom and Della waited, trying their best to remain calm. Mrs. Kemper had come by but had to leave after several hours. They would call her as soon as they had news to share.

The automatic doors swung open and a young man in scrubs came into the room.

"Mancini?" He called out in a firm voice.

Dom went to where the doctor was standing, Della close behind. "I'm Dominic Mancini."

"Mr. Mancini, I'm Dr. Fleishman. I'm a trauma surgeon. Your brother sustained a knife wound and a laceration to his liver. The knife entered his right side, about right here." He pointed to a spot on his torso. "It was a serious wound but we were able to repair it. No other organs were hit. He lost a lot of blood but they got him here quickly." The young physician continued, describing the post-surgical protocol and the fact that the next forty-eight hours would be critical. Dominic retained just one detail: Vinnie was alive. The doctor finished his report. "Do you have any questions?"

"Dr. Fleishman..." Dom took a deep breath. "What are his chances?"

"I won't sugar-coat it, Mr. Mancini. The surgery went well, but a lot of things can go wrong. I'd say his chances are fifty-fifty. As I said, the next forty-eight hours are critical."

They thanked the doctor, marveled at his youth and professionalism, held on to his hand a little too long, and then watched as he turned and exited the way he had entered. Dom and Della fell into each other's arms, tears flowing freely, damp spots collecting on shoulders. For now at least, Vinnie was alive.

———ᴍᴏᴏᴇᴛᴏᴏᴛᴏᴏᴏᴍᴍ———

It was one of those glorious September days in The City, not a cloud in the sky, the temperature expected to reach the low-eighties. The Giants would pack AT&T Park for the umpteenth consecutive sellout and the 49ers were poised to open their season with great expectations. All around town, people shed their jackets and scarves and ties and took their lunches outdoors to the parks, squares, and plazas. Out on the bay, sailboats moved in graceful white clusters around Alcatraz and Angel Island. It was the time of year San Franciscans cherish.

Dominic Mancini had little time to enjoy the season. He was on a mission. He walked all around Union Square, then down Stockton Street past the entrance to Macy's. Nothing there. He made his way back to the Powell Street turntable and waited for a cable car. It was after Labor Day and Dom was able to board without the crush of tourists. The bell rang brightly as the car rolled up the street past the St. Francis Hotel, then farther up the block to the Sir Francis Drake, the doorman standing outside in the traditional British costume. At the crest of Powell Street, passengers jumped off for The Top of the Mark. Soon came the left turn onto Jackson, past the Car Barn and Museum. He looked and listened closely. Still nothing. The car turned right and climbed to the top of Hyde Street where it paused for the magnificent view of Alcatraz and the bay. Some riders stepped off for the photo op while others boarded for the trip down the hill. The car moved forward, tipped dramatically, and down the hill it rolled, intersection after intersection, a long series of steps. Dom could smell the wooden brakes burning as the gripman worked to control the car.

Dom got off at Aquatic Park and looked around. Nothing. He thought about stepping into the Buena Vista for an Irish Coffee, but decided to walk over to Ghirardelli Square instead. As he approached the corner of Beach and Larkin and the stairs that led to the fountain plaza, he saw a small crowd gathered around a street performer and he heard the sound of the alto saxophone.

Dom stood at the back of the crowd and listened. He recognized "Cool Blues" and "Parker's Mood." Vinnie had it right. This man was channeling Charlie Parker.

A song ended and the musician announced he'd be taking a break. People pressed ahead, dropped change and bills into his instrument case, and moved on. Dom stepped forward and smiled as the aged black man poured a cup full of steaming liquid from a thermos bottle. The man paused, lowered his dark glasses, and looked at Dom.

"Well now, there's a familiar face." He wore faded denim pants, battered work boots, and a cable-knit sweater that had no doubt been white once upon a time. A black fisherman's cap covered most of his gray hair.

"Hello." Dom smiled again. "I think you know my brother."

"Well, I'll be damned. Mancini, isn't it?"

"Yes, sir. I'm Dominic." He extended his hand. "Vincent is my brother." They shook hands firmly.

"Ha! Vincent? I always called him Dago Red. No offense."

"None taken. He always called you Bird."

The old man grew serious. "You know, your brother is my hero. Saved a whole day's worth of earnings for me. Ran those kids off and they didn't hardly get a dime." He paused and searched Dom's eyes. "Well now…well, well, well…I am afraid to ask. How is my friend Dago Red?"

Dom felt a lump in his throat, but he managed to get the words out. "He's going to be fine. He'll be coming home in a few days.

We expect him to be back at work by Halloween. Thanksgiving at the latest."

"Oh my, my, my, that is good news. Good news indeed! Tell him Emerson Jones said 'Hello and God bless.'"

"Mr. Jones, would you do me a favor?"

"Why sure. What can I do for you?"

"I want to make a video for Vinnie. Would you play 'Star Eyes'?" Dom took his smart phone from his pocket and opened the camera.

The old man smiled as he picked up his instrument. He moistened his lips, wet the well-trimmed reed, and began to blow.

THE ROYAL ROAD

from *Monday Update*

T he old man's eyes snapped open. He sat bolt upright and threw his legs over the side of the bed. *What in the hell! What was that? And what is this?* He looked down at his lap and saw that he was fully aroused; it had been a very long time. The dream had been vivid, erotic, passionate, and he remembered all of it. Preston Hadley never remembered his dreams. As soon as he awoke, they were gone, erased from memory. *I should write this down. It has to mean something.* But he knew, sitting there on the side of the bed, he didn't need to write anything. He would never forget this dream.

Preston made his way to the bathroom for his morning routine, and from there to the kitchen to brew coffee. As he went through the familiar steps—inserting a fresh filter, scooping coffee grounds, measuring water—his cell phone began to play the tune for a calendar alert. He picked it up and read the display: "Lunch with Melvin." The alert wasn't necessary. He and Melvin Streng met every week at 1:00 p.m. for lunch at the Benicia Yacht Club, unless one of them was out of town or ill. It was Thursday; that meant lunch with Mel.

Preston retrieved the newspaper from the front stoop while Mr. Coffee gurgled away. He had plenty of time to enjoy the morning news, a good cup of Joe, and the summer sunrise. And yet he could not push the dream from his mind. He dropped the paper on the table and stared at the purple bougainvillea in riotous bloom on the wall of his patio.

Jeez, maybe Mel can help me make some sense of this…this damn dream.

Preston drove along 9th Street into the parking lot at Commodore Jones Point. When he was a kid, this was known as Lovers' Point. Now it had been transformed into a park with a monument dedicated to Commodore Thomas Ap Catesby Jones, hero of the war of 1812, founder of the Naval Academy, who once sailed a small fleet into these waters. There was also a boat ramp, busy with fishermen and pleasure boaters putting in at the east end of Southampton Bay. The light morning overcast had burned off quickly and the sun was high in the Northern California sky. The wind was picking up, blowing strong toward the east where it would spin the turbines in the Suisun delta.

He took the yellow rose purchased at the corner market and walked out onto the pier that ran along the right side of the boat ramp. The incoming tide was nearing the high water mark. Looking across the Carquinez Strait to the Contra Costa shore, Preston thought about the happy times spent here with April. God, how he'd loved her. Beautiful, spirited, full of life. When he lost her to a stroke ten years ago, he'd kept his promise to scatter her ashes here at Lovers' Point.

Preston tossed the rose out into the water and watched it drift away to the east. This was his ritual every Thursday, choosing whatever cut flower caught his eye in the market. It was good to spend a few minutes here with April.

He turned and headed back toward his car. Melvin would be waiting for him at the Yacht Club.

Preston greeted Melvin Streng with a smile, a handshake, and a guy hug. Mel had secured their usual table near the window that looked out over the colorful array of boats, sail and power craft of every size and description. Preston went about breaking the bread that had been delivered to their table while Mel poured olive oil into a small saucer and sprinkled it with salt and pepper. They would enjoy the bread and a glass of wine before ordering an entrée. The two men had been friends for twenty years, both of them retired with comfortable pensions, both widowers. Preston would celebrate his seventy-sixth birthday soon, while Mel was a few years younger. Their conversations were generally light and easy, punctuated with laughter. They shared a love of sports and an avid interest in politics, both local and national. But today was different and Mel sensed it right away.

"What's up, Pres? You're not yourself. What's going on?"

"Yeah…well…there is something. Kind of weird, Mel. Are you ready for this?"

"Ready for what, buddy? You've gotta give me a clue." Mel laughed and dipped his bread in the olive oil.

"Okay, here it is. I had a dream this morning. Right before I woke up."

"Yeah, nothing weird about that."

"Except I never remember dreams, Mel. Never. They are gone as soon as my eyes open. Know what I mean?"

Melvin sipped his wine. "But this one you remember?"

"I can't stop thinking about it. I remember every detail."

"Okay, so what was this amazing dream about?" Mel smiled at his friend.

Preston took a deep breath and began. "It was the night before I married April. The wedding party was staying in a large rented house near the beach. I was asleep in a room that had a sofa bed and in the middle of the night, someone came walking through and woke me up. It was Tanya Langley, April's best friend and maid of honor. She went to the kitchen for a glass of water. On her way back, she saw that I was awake and she sat down on the bed to chat. We talked for several minutes. I can't remember what about. Then she laid down next to me and pulled a spare pillow under her head."

"Geez, Pres. Is this goin' where I think it is? And this is April's maid of honor?"

Preston lowered his voice and continued. "Yeah, well…pretty soon I turned toward her and started rubbing her back. She was wearing this long T-shirt with some team logo on the front. And then she threw one leg over mine. And…well, before I could think twice, she was on top of me and we were…you know…together."

"Holy shit, Pres. But wait a minute. This is just a dream, right? This never happened. Did it?"

"No, hell no! I never cheated on April. Not ever. That's why this whole thing is so disturbing. I tell ya, Mel, it's got me shaken up. And I mean bad!"

"Preston, come on. Calm down, buddy. You can't beat yourself up over a damn wet dream." Mel laughed. "Hell, you should be happy that—what are you, seventy-five?—you can still have a sexy dream. Hey, what were you drinking? Maybe I'll try it."

Preston laughed. "I know, I know. It's just that it was so detailed, Mel. I mean, right down to a little gold cross that Tanya wore around her neck, and it was dangling down and resting on my chin and touching my lips. This little gold cross on a very fine chain. I'm tellin' you, Mel, I just can't shake it."

"Hey, it will pass. In a few days you won't remember a thing. Ah, here comes our waiter. Man, I am hungry."

Their waiter brought salads and more wine. The two old friends focused on the food and set the dream aside. For Mel, the case was closed. For Preston, it was front and center, complete with images he could not delete.

Preston sat on the foot of the examining table, shoes removed, shirt unbuttoned, waiting for his cardiologist. There was a light knock on the door, and Dr. Barry Greene entered the small room. "Preston! Good to see you. I can't believe it's been six months. How are you?"

"I'm feelin' great, Barry. But you tell me—how am I?"

They laughed and bantered back and forth while Dr. Greene tapped the keyboard on the wall-mounted platform to display Preston's medical record on the large flat screen. The two men had known each other for a dozen years, since Preston's cardiac bypass surgery, and they'd become friends and occasional golfing partners. The conversation included a brief update on the status of their respective golf games.

"Okay, let's see what we have here." The doctor scanned the results of recent lab tests. "Total cholesterol, one nineteen, beautiful. LDL, good. HDL, good. Triglycerides, good. Sheeh, Preston, I wish all my patients were like this. Are you still going to the gym?"

"Yep, three times a week, sometimes only two. Treadmill, various weight machines. Takes me about an hour."

"Good. Now, take off your shirt and let me listen to you."

Preston removed his shirt and hung it from a hook on the door. He sat on the table while the doctor pressed a stethoscope to his chest and back. Preston lay back on the table to have his abdomen probed and his ankles checked for a robust pulse.

"All right, you can sit up." Dr. Greene again turned his attention to the keyboard and computer screen. "Everything looks good. Let's keep doing what you're doing—the atorvastatin, the atenolol, the low-dose aspirin, regular exercise—and I'll check you again in six months. Okay?"

"Thanks, Barry."

"Any questions for me?" The doctor glanced at his watch. He was on schedule so far this morning, but the appointment calendar was full and it didn't take much to blow it out of the water.

"Yeah, Barry, as a matter of fact I do have one."

Dr. Greene stopped short and turned to his patient. It was rare for Preston to raise a question. "Really? Okay, my friend, shoot."

"Well…it's kind of a strange, but what do you know about dreams? You know, what do they mean, if anything?"

"Dreams? Well damn, Preston, I don't know much. I mean, I studied psychology in school, and we touched on Freud's *The Interpretation of Dreams*—it's a classic—but it's not my field. Why? What's up?"

"I had this dream, Barry. Really disturbing. I can't seem to shake it. I did something terrible—in the dream—something so rotten that I can't deal with it." Preston paused. "Any ideas? I mean, I know this isn't your field, but could you refer me to somebody? Someone who could help me figure this out?"

Preston expected to hear his doctor laugh it off and tell him to take two aspirin and call back in a week, but Barry Greene's face turned serious.

"Hmm, well…here's what I remember, from my days in med school. Freud said, 'Dreams are The Royal Road to the unconscious.' He also said, 'Dreams are all forms of wish fulfillment.' You could fill several volumes with Freud quotations, but those are the two I remember. Now—keep this in mind—Freudian-style psychoanalysis has fallen out of favor. A lot of what Freud said about dreams has been debunked. Frankly, the focus these days is on neuroscience and brain chemistry, what I call 'better living through pharmacology.' You can tell I'm not a fan. Offhand, I can't think of anyone in the area who practices psychoanalysis. But give me a couple of days, let me make some calls. Someone in the office will be in touch. Okay?"

They chatted a while longer, shook hands and said goodbye. Dr. Greene hurried out the door while Preston put on his shirt and reached for his shoes.

Preston opened the cabinet door and reached for the large, white satin-bound album. It had been a very long time since he'd looked at the photos taken the day he and April were married. He sat down in his favorite chair, a glass of red wine on the table within easy reach, and began to turn the pages.

There was April, gorgeous and glowing in a long white gown, her auburn hair swept back in an up-do. There was Preston standing stiffly with his groomsmen, attempting a nervous smile. And then Tanya, handing the bridal bouquet to April, the two of them smiling, their eyes locked. Two beautiful girls, sisters really, lifelong friends, so close they could read each other's thoughts, finish each other's sentences.

Preston's vision clouded as his eyes brimmed. Tears ran down his cheeks and he stifled a sob. He closed the album, unable to look any further, and had a good, long cry—for April, lost to a stroke in her mid-sixties; for his parents and April's, long dead and buried; for himself, alone now nearly ten years. But also for that dream! That damn dream of betrayal that could never be forgiven. He dabbed his eyes with this shirtsleeve and reached for the wine glass.

Tanya. Tanya Langley. How long had it been since he'd heard from her? Had it been since April's funeral? Tanya had married a man named Markenson, someone she'd met in her twenties while traveling through Europe. They'd lived overseas, in France and later in Italy. Tanya and April had kept in touch, exchanging cards and hand-written letters, "old school" communication they called it. They'd reunited a couple of times when Tanya and her husband traveled to San Francisco on business. Preston had missed those visits, for reasons he couldn't recall now. Was Tanya Langley Markenson alive and well? Preston had no idea.

He finished his wine, went to the cabinet and returned the wedding album to its place on the shelf. Preston turned to retrieve the long-stemmed glass for a refill just as his cell phone rang; he pulled it from his pocket and answered the call.

"Hello?"

"Yes, is this Mr. Hadley? Preston Hadley?"

"Yes, who's calling?"

"Mr. Hadley, this is Dr. Greene's office. He asked that we call and let you know that he was able to find the resources you were looking for. I have a short list of names for you."

"Oh...okay. Let me find a pen and paper." Preston wrote the information on a small pad. Judging from the phone numbers, they were all located in the North Bay. "Thank you for calling. And please tell Barry I said thanks."

The woman on the phone reconfirmed his follow-up appointment and said goodbye. Preston dropped the phone back into his pocket and headed toward the kitchen. A second glass of wine was in order.

———✦✦✦———

They sat on the coarse sand at the cove just north of Ft. Ross, Preston's back resting against a half-buried tree trunk, April sitting between his legs, reclining against his chest. His arms were wrapped around her against the chill. They watched the sun as it began its dive into the ocean, a great orange ball, its shape morphing and changing as it seemed to descend into the fog bank a mile or more offshore.

"April, listen to me—" Preston had to find the words, somehow.

"Isn't it beautiful, honey? Have you ever seen a sunset like this?"

"No, I haven't...but listen to me, love. Please, please remember that I love you. More than anything or anyone, more than life—"

"I love you too, babe." She snuggled back into his arms. "Look at those colors. Unbelievable!"

"Just listen, love...I know I will do stupid things, terrible things. But they won't mean anything. Nothing means anything, except I love you. Understand?"

April laughed and cocked her head to look at him. "What are you talking about?" The wind stirred her hair, her cheeks rosy from a day in the sun, not a trace of makeup on her lovely young face. "Let's be still and watch. I want to remember this forever."

Preston drifted back to reality, alone in his room, a distressed old man wide awake in the early morning hours. He reached for his cell phone, pressed the button to light the screen and saw that it was 4:45. Too early to get up, too late to go back to sleep, stranded on this island called a bed with another dream he could never forget.

Melvin Streng waited until 1:20 p.m. Preston was never late, not even once in their long friendship. Mel took his cell phone from his pocket and sent a series of short texts. "Hey, buddy…" "Where are you?" "Didn't forget, did you?" He waited a few minutes. No answer. He called Preston's number and let it ring until it went to voice mail. "Hey, Preston. It's Mel. Everything okay? I'm here at the Yacht Club, at our same old table. Give me a call." At 1:30 he could wait no longer. He dropped some cash on the table and headed for the parking lot.

Mel drove west on K Street toward the intersection with 9th. He knew that Preston stopped by Commodore Jones Point every Thursday to toss a flower into the Carquinez Strait and visit with April. Maybe he was still there. Mel approached the intersection and was surprised to see a beehive of activity and a police barricade across 9th Street, blocking the entrance to the parking lot at the point. He waited in the traffic, now backing up on K. A group of people passed his car, walking east away from the corner. He called out to them.

"Hey…what's going on? Why the road block?"

A young man approached his vehicle. "They say some old guy just walked down the boat ramp, took off his shoes and went into the water. The current caught him and he went under. You know how the tide rips through the strait. He's probably out in Southampton Bay somewhere. Crazy, huh?"

"Yeah, crazy. Thanks." Mel reached the intersection and turned right, heading away from the barricade. It was a short drive to Preston's house. He hoped to find his friend there, safely in his bed, the covers pulled up to his neck, complaining of this, that, or the other. But he couldn't stop his mind from churning. *Some old guy went into the water. Couldn't be. Hell no. Not Preston. Not in a million years. He'd at least call, to talk a little, maybe just to say goodbye. Jeezus, stop it! Don't even think it. It was just some guy. Not Preston. No way. No way in hell.*

It was 1:55 p.m. when he arrived at Preston's place. Mel knocked on the front door, waited a few beats, then rang the doorbell several times. No answer. He had a spare key at home and was about to head for his car to go retrieve it. He tried the door latch. It was unlocked.

"Preston? Hey, Preston! It's Mel. Are you here?" Mel moved slowly through the entryway, into the living room, then down the hall to the bedrooms. Both bedrooms were empty, the beds neatly made. He retraced his steps and went into the kitchen. On the table lay an open Fed Ex envelope and next to it a neatly printed letter. He looked around, called out for Preston again, then let his eyes focus on the letter.

08 September, 2016
Dear Preston,

> I am writing to let you know that my beloved wife, Tanya, passed away last month after a short but gallant battle with cancer. As you know, Tanya thought of you and your late wife, April, as her

dearest friends. As her time grew short, she decided to send certain small items—trinkets, pieces of jewelry—to people she loved, something they could hold to remember her by. The memento in the velvet pouch (enclosed) is for you.

I regret that we never met, though I had the privilege of meeting April on two memorable occasions in San Francisco. I hope this letter finds you in good health. Perhaps I will have the pleasure of meeting you one day soon, before our journeys end.

Fondly,

Anthony A. Markenson

Melvin moved the letter aside. Beneath it was a small black velvet pouch. He lifted it from the table and let the contents spill out. He caught his breath and his eyes welled as he stared at the small gold cross on a very fine chain.

EXECUTIVE SWEET

A One-act Play

from *Monday Update*

C haracters (in order of appearance):
Brianna Brubaker: receptionist
Dirk Stonebreaker: job applicant
Barton Q (Bart) Crumley: businessman
Abby Lovelace: attorney

Scene:

> *The reception area of the executive offices of BQC International, a high-tech product development and marketing firm, situated on the seventh floor of a luxury high-rise office building in Silicon Valley. At stage left are twin elevators, the doors a burnished gold finish. At center stage, a modern executive-size desk equipped with recessed computer monitors and a telephone exchange panel. At stage right, modern chairs, a couch and table, all in a minimalist style, covered in rich black leather. Behind the desk are floor-to-ceiling doors that lead to the executive suite of offices. The walls are paneled in polished oak and hung with prints in the Impressionist style. On one of the walls, in large gold figures, is the logo for BQC International.*

[*As the scene opens, the receptionist (Brianna Brubaker) is opening and sorting a large stack of mail. She is in her early thirties, well-dressed, well-groomed, and quite attractive. Her actions are swift, efficient and confident, befitting the gatekeeper to the executive suite. A bell sounds and a man (Dirk Stonebreaker) steps off one of the elevators, looking around quizzically. He is tall, sandy haired, and exhibits a noticeable paunch. His suit is of discount store quality and it no longer fits; the jacket cannot be buttoned across his belly. His shoes are worn at the heels and haven't been polished in recent memory. He approaches the receptionist's desk.*]

DIRK: Hi there! [*He smiles cheerfully*] How are you today?

BRIANNA: I am fine, thank you. [*She returns his smile, somewhat cautiously.*] How can I help you?

DIRK: The name is Stonebreaker...Dirk Stonebreaker. I have an appointment for a job interview at 1:15 p.m. [*He checks his watch*] I'm a little early.

BRIANNA: Oh, well, I'm afraid you have the wrong floor. Human Resources is located on the fifth floor. This is the seventh, the executive offices.

DIRK: Oh...my bad. Just down two floors, right? [*He glances toward the elevator*]

BRIANNA: That is correct.

DIRK [*giving her the once-over*]: Say, Miss...what did you say your name was?

BRIANNA: I didn't. It's Brubaker. Brianna Brubaker.

DIRK: Well, Miss Brubaker...are all the ladies here at BQC International as pretty as you? *[He flashes his most charming smile.]*

BRIANNA: I really can't comment on "all the ladies" here at BQC. And it is Mrs. Brubaker.

[She places her elbows on the desk, folding her hands under her chin so that he can see the exquisite ring set on her left hand.]

DIRK: Hey, I won't tell anybody if you won't. What say I buy you a drink after my interview?

BRIANNA: Fifth floor, Mr. Stonebreaker. And while you're there, ask them for a copy of our sexual harassment policy. I'm sure you'll find it interesting.

[The door to the executive suite opens and a man (Bart Crumley) walks out. He is of medium height with the trim build of a distance runner. His flaming red hair is neatly cut and styled. He is wearing expensive loafers, well-tailored slacks, and a polo shirt bearing the BQC logo.]

BART: Brianna, please let me know as soon as Abby arrives. We have a date for lunch. *[He glances at Dirk and smiles.]* Hello. Can we help you? Oh...but I'm sure Brianna has taken care you.

[The two men stare at each other. There is a spark of recognition.]

BART: Dirk? Dirk Stonebreaker? Is that you?

DIRK: Oh my God...I don't believe this. Bugs? Bugs Crumley! How long has it been? It's got to be ten...no, twelve years. Since we graduated from Vallejo High School.

[The two men come together and shake hands firmly. They stand to the right of the desk, Dirk closest to Brianna who is slightly behind him.]

BART: So, Dirk, how are you and what have you been up to?

DIRK: Doing great, Bugs. Just great. I'm in sales, automotive mostly. Been doing it off and on since...well since a year or two after high school.

BRIANNA *[audible only to Dirk]*: Automotive...as in used cars, no doubt.

BART: I thought you got a football scholarship, to one of those southern powerhouse schools. LSU, wasn't it?

DIRK: Yeah...well...that didn't work out so well. I blew out a knee during spring practice...a torn ACL...and they eventually pulled my scholarship.

BART: Oh...sorry to hear that, Dirk. I always thought you'd wind up in the NFL, maybe play for the 49ers. That would have been something.

DIRK *[anxious to change the subject]*: Yeah...me too. But say, Bart, you're looking great! How about you? What did you do after high school?

BART: I went to MIT, earned a degree in electronic engineering. Then I came back to the West Coast and got my MBA at Stanford.

DIRK *[rather deflated]*: Really? Well...you always were a brainiac...a real geek. No offense.

[He laughs uncomfortably.] Hey, do you remember when you were equipment manager for the varsity football team?

BART *[with a frozen smile]*: How could I forget?

DIRK *[laughing loudly]*: I guess we were a little hard on you.

BART: You might say that.

DIRK: Hey, remember that time *[he pauses to laugh]* when we were on that road trip, and we convinced Coach and the bus driver that everyone was on the bus while you were still in the men's room?

BART *[laughing too, in spite of the painful memory]*: Yeah, and the bus pulled out without me. Left me there in that diner in the middle of nowhere.

DIRK *[trying to control his laughter]*: Oh, wow! And you'd probably still be there except that one of the guys wimped out and told Coach. He made the bus driver turn around and go back for you.

BRIANNA *[to Dirk]*: Let me guess…you were not the one who wimped out. True?

BART: Ah, but my personal favorite was the night when you and your friends pantsed me…including my underwear…and left me on the quad in back of the main building.

DIRK: Oh my God! I forgot about that. What did you do?

BART: Well, luckily there was a basketball game that night in the gym, so I figured I could get into my locker, put on my gym shorts, and call my parents for a ride home.

DIRK: Good thinking.

BART: First, I went to the dumpster by the cafeteria and found an empty cardboard box to put over my head while I ran through the lobby of the gym, you know, where the concession stand and the ticket takers' table was located.

DIRK: Yeah…what happened?

BART: Well, I made it into the locker room, got my gym shorts and used the coaches' office to make the phone call. Then I came out to the lobby to wait.

DIRK: So it worked? You got away without being recognized?

BART: Not really. People in the lobby started laughing and saying, "Nice try, red."

[Dirk is convulsed with laughter now. Brianna is shaking her head, a disgusted look on her face.
A bell rings, the elevator doors open and a woman (Abby Lovelace) steps into the reception area. She is a tall and elegant brunette, dressed in a beautifully tailored navy blue suit and white blouse. The skirt ends just above the knee and reveals her lovely calves, the toned muscles evident as she strides toward the desk in a pair of navy Jimmy Choo pumps. She waves to Brianna, continues directly to Bart and plants a brief but very affectionate kiss on his lips.]

ABBY [turning to look at Dirk]: Hello, sorry to interrupt…Oh my God! [her face registers shock]…Dirk Stonebreaker! I can't believe this.

DIRK [giving Abby an up-and-down assessment]: Well, hello there. Do we know each other?

BART: Dirk, this is Abby Lovelace. Remember? She was in our graduating class. Class valedictorian.

DIRK: Oh yeah…you were the girl we called—

ABBY [with a stone-cold stare]: "Flabby Love-less." Yes, I remember.

BRIANNA [to Dirk]: My, oh my, such a charmer.

DIRK [starts to laugh, then catches himself]: Yeah, well…you know how we were…back in those days.

ABBY: I sure do. I'll never forget the time you taped that sign on my back as I was coming out of the cafeteria. What did it say? Oh yes, I remember: "Wide Load."

DIRK [a little embarrassed and defensive now]: Hey, that wasn't my idea. Gary Dickman made the sign. I just…uh…stuck it on your back.

BRIANNA [sarcastically]: Oh, well in that case—

ABBY: I wore that sign most of the day, until one of my friends removed it.

DIRK [trying desperately to change the subject]: Abby, you look great now! No more Flabby Abby. [He laughs.]

ABBY: And you, Dirk. You've certainly—shall we say—filled out?

DIRK [absent-mindedly patting his belly]: Yeah…well—

BRIANNA: Oooo…now the sign is on the other back.

DIRK [trying to ignore Brianna]: So...Abby, what are you doing these days?

ABBY: I'm an attorney. Stanford Law, Class of 2010.

DIRK: A lawyer? Ya don't say...

BART: And, get this, Dirk: Abby and I are engaged! [He holds up Abby's left hand to display a lovely five-carat diamond ring.]

DIRK [looking at the ring]: Holy crap!

BART: Abby is representing BQC in the preparations for an IPO. Of course, once we're married, she'll hand off those responsibilities. [He turns to Abby and they smile warmly at one another.]

BRIANNA [to Dirk]: Just gets better and better, doesn't it?

BART: But, Dirk, tell me: what brings you here today?

DIRK: Oh, yeah...I have a job interview...[he glances at his watch] coming up in a few minutes. I'm up for a position in sales. I hear this is a top notch outfit—growing like crazy. I figure they could use a man like me.

BRIANNA [almost suppressing a laugh]: Snork!

DIRK: How about you, Bugs? I see you're wearing a company logo shirt. Do you work here?

BART: Yeah, I guess you could say that. BQC stands for Barton Q Crumley. It is my company. I own it. [He pauses.] At least for the time being, until the IPO. Then it will belong to the shareholders.

DIRK *[his face fallen, in shock]:* Ya don't say—

BART: Listen, Dirk…*[He grabs Dirk's hand and shakes it firmly.]* it's been great seeing you. Abby and I are off to lunch. Good luck down in HR. *[He pauses for a broad smile, Abby at his side.]* It would be interesting having *you* working for *me*.

[Bart and Abby head for the elevator, arm in arm, talking softly and laughing. The elevator doors open and they disappear.]

BRIANNA: Well now, I think that went quite well, don't you?

DIRK *[glaring at Brianna]:* Hey, you've sure got a smart mouth… for a receptionist. *[He puts air quotes around "receptionist."]*

BRIANNA *[laughing]:* Yes, well, after the IPO, with all my stock options, I'll be known as Brianna Brubaker – Millionaire Receptionist. *[She mimics his air quotes.]*

DIRK *[turning toward the elevator]:* Ah, geez—

BRIANNA: Oh, Mr. Stonebreaker…one question…

DIRK *[pausing, turning toward her]:* Yeah?

BRIANNA: Do you like to read?

DIRK: Yeah, sometimes.

BRIANNA: There is a new book out that I think you might enjoy. It is a fresh translation of well-known bible verses, intended for modern times.

DIRK: Yeah, so?

BRIANNA: There is one in particular I think you will appreciate. Matthew 5:5: "Blessed are the Geeks, for they shall inherit the earth." *[She gives Dirk a warm smile.]*

[Dirk turns, mumbling, and enters the elevator. As the doors close and the lights dim, Brianna is heard singing softly to herself.]

BRIANNA: *We're in the money / We're in the money / We got a lotta what it takes to get along…*

The End

But for the Grace of God

from *Monday Update*

The display on your phone says "Unknown" and you know better, but you go ahead and answer. Sure enough, it's Dave Dunk and you barely say hello before he launches into his monologue.

"Hey, Cory, listen I was talking to Detrick the other day, you know he came and bailed me out of the hospital in Vacaville, they wouldn't let me out because I'm on medication and they say I could have an accident and sue the hospital, so I says how the hell am I gonna get outta here, and this nurse tells me somebody is gonna have to sign me out, so I'm thinking who can I call, and I'm thinking Delmonico cause Kent and I grew up together, Federal Terrace, we were neighbors, a good friend. Remember Kent? How about his sister Renee? Beautiful girl, dark hair, Sophia Loren, am I right? Anyway, Kent's not home. So I call Detrick and he comes up and signs me out and wheels me out to my car. Isn't that a good thing to do, Cory, a good friend?"

"Yeah, Dave, listen—" You want to tell him that you can't talk right now but it's no use.

"So I bought seven dozen copies of your book, Cory, and sent one to Ben Hanes, you know he lives in Buena Park, and he says he loves the book but you should have kept all the real names in there, know what I mean? But I'm telling you, Cory, take your book and go to Mare Island, and they have this book fair and you set up a table and you could sell a lot of copies, know what I mean? So Detrick gets me out of the hospital and I've got about four grand on me from a settlement and I say let's go have a drink, but he says he's got to get back to Vallejo, but that's a nice thing he did, don't you think, Cory? So I'm talking to Nate Carp and I'm telling him about you and he says he remembers you, that little chubby guy who threw ninety miles an hour (laughter), and I says yeah I played behind him for five years, never got a ground ball, never got a pop-up, nobody ever hit the ball (laughter), and he says whatever happened to that guy, but you know how great Carp was, six three, two hundred pounds, throw the ball through a brick wall, all of the above, and his brother Don, thirty-three touchdowns his senior year, greatest athlete ever to come out of Vallejo…"

And on and on it goes, and you wonder how you are going to get out of this conversation without simply hanging up, and maybe that's exactly what you should do.

"…and my parents bought that house over on the east side of the freeway and I'm this little ragamuffin from the projects and you guys have this neighborhood and it's like Ozzie & Harriet'ville, am I right, Cory? (laughter) So I was signed by the Twins out of Vallejo J.C., no help from Coach McMillan who hated my guts. I was signed by Billy Martin, remember Billy Martin, ex-Yankee, World Series MVP, best friends with Mickey Mantle, Billyball, so I go to Rookie Ball and I tear it up, hit .400, a dozen homeruns, good leather, but they've got no money invested in me, Cory, so I keep getting passed over by guys with big bonuses, including a guy I roomed with, Rod Carew, Rod was my roommate, I used to call him Snowball, and the guy could hit, am I right? Hall of Fame, flirted with .400 every year, all of the above…"

And it's been about thirty minutes now and you really don't have time for this, so you try to break in. "Dave! Hey, Dave! Listen, I've got to get off the line."

"Okay, Cory, before I stop boring you, you remember my brother Claude? He was a great artist, am I right? Good athlete, great hitter, threw blocks for Don Carp when he scored thirty-three touchdowns his senior year, my brother hasn't spoken to me in twenty years. Can you believe that, Cory? So my brother did this cartoon, you remember he was an artist, and it shows this guy standing on first base next to the first baseman, and the first baseman has a hole through his cap, this ragged jagged hole right through one side of his cap, and the first baseman says to the guy on first base, 'Nice hit, Lefty.' Get it? 'Nice hit, Lefty!' So I take my brother's cartoon and I blow it up and I make it about twenty-four by thirty-six inches, and the detail is incredible, Cory, the uniforms, the baselines, the grass, the fence, the foul pole, all of the above, I blow it up to look like a limited edition print and I frame it for my brother. Of course he doesn't want it, so it hangs in my parents' house for twenty years, remember my parents, Cory? Came to all the games, right? So it's there for twenty years and when my parents pass away my sister sells off all the stuff in the house and she gives this framed piece to Theo Demopolis. You know Demopolis, right, Cory?"

"Yeah, Theo is a friend of mine."

"So Demopolis is a big shot with the Theatre Guild, right? So he uses this piece as a prop for some plays, and this piece is worth something to me, Cory, I mean it's probably worth twenty-five large, because my brother is a known artist and my sister who hates my guts has no business giving it away. Am I right, Cory?"

"Yeah, but Dave, why are you telling me—"

"And I'm thinking since you're friends with Demopolis, you can talk to him and get it back. Know what I mean, Cory? Would he talk to you? Could you do that for me?"

And there it is. How can you say no to that? He's pulled you in again. So you say *yes* and then the monologue rolls on through nearly everyone you ever knew while growing up in Vallejo, the rich, the poor, the famous, and the infamous. Dave knew them all and he gives you a capsule comment on every single one, and it's the same every time he calls. You could lay the phone down and walk away and come back twenty minutes later and he'd never know it. And you promise yourself that someday you're going to try that—just lay the phone down and see how long it takes him to notice.

"So you'll call Demopolis for me, Cory? Can you do that?"

And before he can launch another monologue, you shout him down, assure him you'll reach out to Theo, and then you hang up. And now you feel like crap for cutting him off because you know the guy has had health issues recently, something to do with a faulty pacemaker that required surgery and resulted in an infection. That was in Reno last year, but now this hospital stay in Vacaville, what was that all about?

The funny thing is you remember that damn cartoon Dave is talking about. You spent the night at his house after the last game of the season when you were thirteen, Scofield's vs. All Stars. It was the only time you stayed over there, and you remember that his brother had all kinds of sketches and drawings and stuff plastered all over the walls of the room they shared. And there was that cartoon: "Nice hit, Lefty." Did Dave really blow it up, turn it into a print and have it framed? You never know how much to believe. Maybe he's cooked up the whole thing in his head. You'll reach out to Theo, ask him if he knows anything about it. Theo's a good guy, a straight-shooter. You'll call Theo later.

———✦———

It's a day or two later and you send an e-mail to Theo. He replies right away and you're shocked to find there really is a framed print. Theo has it, and just like Dave said, his sister gave it to Theo when the senior Dunks passed away. Theo gives you some background and makes it clear that he'd be happy to get rid of the damn thing, as long as Dave Dunk won't be coming to his door. So you reach out to Detrick and he says yeah, he'll go to Theo's place and pick it up and see that Dave gets it.

You ask Detrick about bailing Dave out of the hospital and he fills you in. Apparently Dave has severe gout and he can barely walk. Detrick has some bad history with Dave, but he also remembers when they were kids in elementary school and lived a few doors from each other. You're amazed at what a good, forgiving guy Detrick is, because you know the bad history.

The worst Dave ever did to you was to call at 3:00 a.m. and ask you to come bail him out of the drunk tank, and that was a long, long time ago. And your wife told you if you go bail that bozo out of jail to just keep going. So you didn't go. Dave was released the next day. End of story.

Now you've made the arrangements and you're feeling better about things, so you call Dave to tell him. Fortunately, you get his voice mail and you leave him a message. You have an e-mail address too, so you send him a message, and then you say to yourself *well, that's that.*

Yeah, right.

———✤———

A couple of days go by and then the phone calls start. You see "Unknown" flash on your iPhone screen and you let it go to voice mail and it's always some variation on the same theme. You thought the issue of the framed print was closed, but it's not closed in Dave Dunk's mind. You make it a point to turn off your cell phone at night. When you turn it back on, you're amazed at some of the time stamps. He's left messages as early as 5:30 a.m. And the monologue rolls on and on:

"Yeah, Cory, I'm gonna be in Sausalito for the next week, then I'm going to Florida for the winter. I can't get ahold of Detrick about that print, but I'll be here for the rest of the week, so give me a call at 775-555-5555."

"775-555-5555, yeah, Cory, I'll be at the Marriott at Jack London Square for the rest of the week, then I'm flying out to

Palm Springs. Hey, I'll pay that guy, you know what I mean, for that print. And I sent something to you at the address on Russell but it came back, so I need your address. So get back to me."

"Yeah, Cory, 775-555-5555, I'm leaving for Florida on Monday, but you're gonna get a call from a friend of mine in Vegas, his name is Tony Salinas, he's gonna call you about your book. Anyway, I'm leaving for Florida on Monday, so get back to me."

You finally call him back and you get his voice mail, so you reiterate the message: Detrick is going to pick up the print from Theo, and you're sure that he'll be in touch, and just go ahead and enjoy the winter in Florida. Or Palm Springs. Or wherever.

Dave leaves one more message and he's thrilled that you called him back, and it makes you feel like a real jerk for not taking his calls. "775-555-5555, hey, Cory, thanks for calling me back, and hey, there's no hurry. I mean how can there be a hurry between us? I mean I've known you for sixty years, man. And I talked to Delmonico the other day, first time in twenty years, and you and him, you're like idols to me, you guys are the best, and you know what, his grandson plays football now, has had five carries and scored five touchdowns! Isn't that something? So thanks, Cory, for making that call for me, and Tony Salinas is gonna call you."

Listening to the messages is exhausting—utterly, totally exhausting. But it wasn't always like this, especially if you go way back, back to when you were kids growing up in Vallejo and playing baseball together. You remember when Dave's family moved to the house on Miller, just east of the freeway, coming out of federal housing. He was a good ballplayer, damn good, and he had great hands and lots of style and attitude, and you liked him right away. Then he was drafted onto your Little League team and you were league champs that year. That's when you were twelve. And you played together again when you were thirteen and what a year that was—an undefeated season. God what fun! And you remember Dave and Artie coming over to your house and you'd hike out to East Vallejo Little League and take batting practice for hours. Just three guys, that's all you needed—a hitter, a pitcher, and a guy to shag balls in the outfield—and you could practice all day if you wanted to. And then head over to the Auto Movies and break a board in the fence and mess around on the playground down by the screen. And the maintenance guy who worked out there would come and chase you out. What a way to kill a summer day. But it was more than baseball. Dave liked you and you liked him and he was funny as hell and he always made you laugh. Except for the time the three of you—Dave, Artie, and you—got caught shoplifting Hershey Bars from the Safeway store. That's a night you'd just as soon forget. And what about when you and Dave were bat boys for Legion Post 550? You got to travel with the team, and what a great team it was, with Nate Carp, and Lee, and Augie, and Larry, and Dave's brother. And then later, you and Dave played high school and legion ball together.

But there was nothing like those summer days when you were thirteen, hiking out to East Vallejo with your bat, your glove, your spikes, and a bag of beat up baseballs. It was great being a kid and having friends like that. And that was Dave, and that's why you answer his calls from time to time, and that's why you let him suck you in again and again.

You know that the root of the problem is alcohol. You think about your friends, good friends, the best friends a guy could ever have, and you make a mental list of the ones with drinking problems. There was Ray who eventually destroyed his life, and you remember the two of you trying over and over again to mix the perfect Manhattan. And there's Darin who was like a brother to you, and now he's in a group home, his liver ruined, waiting to die. And there's Brent who calls you when he's had a few rum-and-cokes and tells you that his daughter is worried about his drinking, and asks you if he should be worried too. And of course there's good old Dave Dunk.

You have to ask yourself if you are edging your way onto that list. *Take a look in the mirror, buddy boy.* But you can handle it.

You can function without it. Just to prove it, you're not going to take a drink for the next two weeks. Okay, make it one week.

Geez, who the hell are you kidding?

You know damn well it's a tightrope: all the well-adjusted social drinkers and non-drinkers on one side, and all the alcoholics on the other. And how many people do you know who are up on that high wire trying to keep their balance? You think about Dave, and Ray, and Darin, and Brent, and you know it's true, undeniable, irrefutable, carved in stone, and so you say it out loud: "There but for the grace of God…"

RADICAL DANCER
from *Monday Update*

I turned left off University Avenue, then right onto Hearst. A block or so east, I pulled to the curb and looked across the street toward the apartment building. The street number was correct, but the old building had been taken down and a new one stood in its place. This was the address where I'd lived with Natalia.

Natalia Meyerson. Oh my God, what a girl! Her given name was Ann, but she went by Natalia because she thought it sounded Russian. She was a dancer. It's what she lived for it, not just the physical act but the creation. She dreamt of becoming a renowned choreographer. Her great passion was to create interpretive pieces for a local dance company. She would select a piece of music— anything from Debussy to Ellington to Milhaud—create a dance, and then have me sit on the couch in her living room, the lights low, the volume high, while she perfected the routine. She danced in the nude, always, the greatest turn-on I'd ever experienced, seared into my memory. To this day, I can close my eyes and there she is, moving with sweeping abstract grace across the bare hardwood floor of her apartment.

If I stand up nice and straight, I might reach five ten. Natalia stood at least two inches taller. Her long legs were beautifully formed and toned by hours of practice. I wasn't a "leg man" until I met Natalia. Those legs renewed my faith in the existence of God. The rest of the portrait fit perfectly. Narrow hips and a hard little ass. Perky breasts that never required a bra. Short dark hair cut in a pixie style and large, dark eyes, like the subject of a Keene painting. Her nose was a little too long, a slight imperfection. But the sum of all those parts was stunning. I was crazy about Natalia.

And then she dumped me.

I was back in Berkeley, California, for a short consulting assignment, my first time in the East Bay since the late sixties. I pulled away from the curb, heading east to find the Shattuck Plaza Hotel. After settling into my room, I decided to see if any of my old colleagues were still living in the area. I found the phone book on the shelf of the nightstand and Regan Criswell's name jumped off the page. He answered my call with the familiar raspy voice I remembered so well and suggested we meet at Starbucks on Oxford Street, a short walk from the hotel.

———⁓∽ᴏᴄᴏↄᴏᴏↄᴏᴏᴏ⁓———

I recognized Regan as soon as he opened the door at Starbucks. It had been forty-five years since I'd seen him, but no matter. He still had the full beard and the lush head of hair, both gone gray now. But the thing that triggered recognition was the merry twinkle in his eyes. You don't forget something like that and there it was, intact after all the years.

Regan didn't see me, at least not at first. He approached a gray-haired man sitting at a small table and I heard him say, "Carl, is that you?" The man looked at him in total surprise and started to respond just as I clamped a hand on Regan's shoulder and said, "Excuse me. Has anyone seen Regan Criswell around here?"

He spun around and gathered me in a bear hug. "Ha! Carl Stenson! How the hell are ya?"

I hugged him back and the laughter and conversation started to roll, even before we could find an open table or think about ordering coffee.

Regan was one of those people you never forget, no matter

how many years have passed. We were both in our seventies now and the chaotic Berkeley of the mid- to late-sixties seemed very far away. Back in the day, we'd been employed at Lawrence Radiation Laboratory, high up on the hill behind the UC Berkeley campus. I was a computer operator in the data center, and Regan was an expeditor for the physics group headed by Dr. Luis Alvarez. He worked as the middle man between the data center and the Alvarez Group, assembling the data and designating the programs to process the results of the experiments conducted on the Lab's high-energy particle accelerators. I worked the graveyard shift— midnight to eight—and would see Regan most every night as he came in to deliver a new batch of work and pick up the results of prior processing. He was a favorite among the operations crew, always with a new adventure to share. We had engaged Regan in some great discussions during my years at the Rad Lab.

I had a question for my old friend. "So tell me, Regan, are you still into chemical mind expansion?" He'd been notorious for trying every drug he could get his hands on, and in Berkeley in the sixties, the choices seemed endless.

"Nah, man, no way." He laughed at the suggestion. "I gave that up a long time ago."

"Yeah? What happened?"

"Too many bad trips, man. And I mean *bad!*"

His eyes sparkled as I reminded him how he used to regale us with tales of LSD and hash and Quaaludes. As for marijuana, that was like a cup of coffee, just a way to start the day. Name a drug and Regan Criswell could tell you all about it.

We launched into a discussion of the Berkeley we remembered from those days. Mario Savio and the Free Speech Movement, which morphed into the Anti-Vietnam War Movement. The endless demonstrations in Sproul Plaza. Marches down Telegraph Avenue. The Black Panther Party headquartered over in Oakland. And People's Park. God, who could forget People's Park and Bloody Thursday? What a place, what a time!

"Regan, remember that night we came to work and the guys told us about the police helicopter that dropped tear gas on Sproul Plaza?"

"Hell yes, I remember. Geez, can you picture that happening today?"

"Ha! There'd be ten thousand videos posted on You Tube, Tweets trending around the world, pictures posted on Instagram. Can you imagine Mario Savio's Facebook page?" We laughed hard over that thought.

The conversation raged on until I had to break in and excuse myself. I had an appointment to get to. We took our coffees and exited the shop, lingering for just a minute on the sidewalk.

"Just before I left the Lab, Regan, you were in the process of buying a boat. Am I right?"

"Yeah, a sloop. Man, what a thing of beauty. Needed a lot of work, so I got it dirt cheap."

"Weren't you going to live on it? Down at the marina?"

"I *did* live on it. For about six months." He paused. "You know, Natalia lived with me on the boat."

He gave me a sly smile. I didn't know what to say. After Natalia and I went our separate ways, I'd heard she and Regan were dating. On that strange note, we shook hands and agreed to meet again while I was in town. I was a little rattled as I headed for my appointment.

Later on, as I relaxed in my hotel room, the phone rang. It was Regan suggesting we meet for dinner the next evening at Chez Panisse. I couldn't wait to continue our conversation.

———

Chez Panisse, Alice Waters's iconic restaurant, lived up to its impeccable reputation, worthy of all the stars it had been awarded. The sommelier selected an appropriate wine to accompany each course and by the time we were ready for desert, I was flying high.

So was Regan, though it didn't affect his rapid-fire speech and the endless stream of stories. All I had to do was pose a question and he was off and running. But Regan had a question of his own.

"So, Carl, why did you and Natalia break up? I asked her once but she didn't want to talk about it."

"Well, I guess you could say it was politics. Crappy reason, isn't it? You know how she was into all the radical movements around town. First it was the Free Speech thing. Then Vietnam. Then People's Park. And civil rights. She was always dragging me to some meeting or some protest march. I was for civil rights, but not the rest of it. I didn't believe in 'the cause,' whatever the friggin' cause happened to be at the moment. I thought the Free Speech people were a bunch of spoiled kids who didn't appreciate the education their parents were paying for. I thought the U.S. was right to be in Vietnam. And People's Park? I thought the University was right. Hell, I thought Governor Reagan did the right thing, cracking down, calling out the National Guard."

"Holy crap, Carl. No wonder she kicked you out." Regan had a good laugh at my expense.

"What about you? How did you handle all that *activism*?"

"Oh, I was anti-war all right. You remember the discussions we used to have up in the computer center. I didn't care about the rest of it. But I went with Natalia to all the meetings and rallies and demonstrations." He gave me the wry smile again. "Hell, I just wanted to watch her dance."

I knew exactly what he meant.

We finished our desserts, and I signaled to the waiter for more coffee. I would need several cups before heading back to the hotel. I turned to see Regan staring at me.

"You know…I have a story to tell you that you won't believe."

"Oh yeah? Let's hear it." Regan had my attention now.

"Remember that night, March of 1968, when some 'urban guerillas' bombed the power line that fed the Radiation Lab?"

"Of course I remember. I was working that night. Everything

45

went black, all the systems went down, even the air handlers. Dead quiet. The only lights were the battery-powered lanterns mounted on the walls, and half of them didn't work. We sat there all night. I think around 4:00 a.m. a security guy came in to tell us the power line had been bombed."

"Yeah, well, I was there." Regan cracked an embarrassed grin.

"You mean in the computer center? I don't remember seeing you that night."

"No. I mean I was there. Where the power line was bombed."

"What? You're shitting me!"

"Nope. Natalia and I went to a meeting that night. It was all about how Lawrence Radiation Lab was supporting weapons development and supporting the war effort and on and on like that. Then we went with a couple of guys to an apartment in Berkeley. I was smoking some damn fine pot and I was higher than shit. We piled into an old VW van and hit the road, out through the Caldecott Tunnel. And then we were on a dirt road out in the grazing lands. I remember seeing cows. At least I think I saw cows. And the two guys jumped out and started rigging some packages to a tower on the power line. Natalia climbed into the driver's seat. We made another stop and they did the same on another tower. And I'm sittin' there trying to figure what the hell is going on."

"Jeezus, what then?"

"The guys jumped back in, Natalia driving, and we hauled ass back to the main road. And then BLAM! There was an explosion. And that's it. End of story."

I sat there staring at Regan Criswell in shock and disbelief. My old friend—an urban guerilla. And Natalia drove the getaway van! I had no words.

Regan called for our check. His tale put a chill on the conversation. Our evening was over. I declined his offer of a ride back to the hotel, saying I preferred to walk. It was only a mile. I needed some time to clear my head.

Back in my room, I opened my laptop and connected to the hotel's WiFi. I started searching for news reports of the bombing, expecting to find full accounts from the *Oakland Tribune* and the *San Francisco Chronicle*. Nothing turned up from those two heavyweights, but I found a clip from a newspaper in Lodi:

> Saturday, March 23, 1968: Earlier this week, a bomb toppled a 115,000 volt power line cutting power to LRL Berkeley…Another damaged tower on the same line was discovered…Friday's blast, March 22, included three charges of plastic explosive, only one of which detonated.

I searched a while longer but could find no other reports. Apparently no one had ever been arrested for the crime. Less than two weeks later, April 4, 1968, Martin Luther King was assassinated. It seemed the bombing story got buried; there were bigger problems to deal with. I gave up searching and closed the laptop.

———～w∽∽∞⊙↶⊙↷∞∽∽w———

Regan and I met one more time before I left Berkeley, back at the Starbucks on Oxford. We chatted for a while about nothing in particular, but I had one more question for him.

"What about Natalia? Did she stay around Berkeley?"

"Not for long. She gave up dance. Went to law school in San Francisco. Graduated from Hastings in 1980."

"How did she manage that?"

"Family money, Carl. She could do whatever she wanted. Practiced under her real name—Ann Meyerson. She was in the public defender's office for a long time, then joined a firm that did personal injury law. Ann won some major malpractice cases against hospitals and doctors. Believe me, the American Medical Association knew her name."

"Did you stay in touch?"

"We talked on the phone a few times. I went to see her argue a case once. You should have seen her, Carl. Tall, erect, that dancer's posture, those beautiful legs coming out of a perfectly tailored suit. She was regal. And she was damn good."

"Yeah, I'll bet. Is she still in The City?"

Regan looked away. When he turned toward me, the merriment was gone from his eyes.

"She passed away a couple of years ago. I thought you knew, Carl."

"No, I didn't know. I'm so sorry." I didn't know what else to say, so I said it again. "I'm so sorry."

We talked a while longer but there wasn't much left to say. We embraced one last time, and said goodbye.

———ᴡᴡᴏᴏᴄ₎ᴇᴛᴏ₍ᴇᴛᴏ₎ᴏᴏᴡᴡ———

I drove down University Avenue heading for the freeway that would take me to the Oakland Airport. I had some time to spare so I continued on University into the Berkeley Marina and parked along Marina Boulevard. The view of San Francisco and the bridges was spectacular, especially the new eastern span of the Bay Bridge, a soaring single tower suspension leaping from Oakland to Yerba Buena Island. I could remember standing on the balcony of the administration building fifty years ago, up on the hill above the campus, drinking in the view. I turned to look back toward the Campanile Tower and the hills beyond. At that moment, the past seemed like a dream, a time and place that could not have been real.

Did any of it really happen?

It was time for a reality check. I pulled my cell phone from my pocket and called home. Allison answered, her voice bright and cheery.

"Hi, babe. You headed for the airport?" I could tell she was smiling.

"Yeah, just about to leave The Peoples' Republic of Berkeley."

She laughed. "How did it go?"

"Work was fine. But, kind of a strange week. I'll tell you all about it when I get home."

"Okay. I'm making the marinara that you love. Thought we'd have some pasta, a nice salad. I'll pick up a baguette, maybe a good Cabernet. How's that sound?"

"Like heaven. I'll see you soon." I paused for a moment. "Alli…I love you."

"I love you too, Carl. Have a good flight."

I left the marina and merged onto the freeway heading south toward the airport. I could picture Allison, at home in our kitchen, working over her marinara, humming a happy tune, NPR on the radio in the background. I am a firm believer in karma, and I had to ask myself the question: What had I ever done to be so blessed?

THE BIG TOMATO

"Sacramento is a city with a colorful history,
from the Gold Rush to the Pony Express
to the transcontinental railroad,
not to mention the famous and infamous politicians
who made reputations there in state government.
Out in the tree-lined suburbs, it is known
as a good place to raise a family,
and close to everything—the mountains,
Lake Tahoe, the coast, San Francisco.
In all the ways to describe Sacramento,
the words 'pretty' or 'beautiful'
never come into play."

-C.W.S. from *Children of Vallejo*

"I think L.A. or San Francisco could be rushed,
but Sacramento is just laid back."

-Nick Johnson

AND SPARE THEM NOT

from *Monday Update*

Max Silver loved the little piece of ground he called his tomato patch. Situated in one corner of his backyard, it wasn't much more than eight feet wide by twelve feet long, but the production every year amazed him. Maybe it was the late morning and early afternoon sun, or the yards and yards of steer manure he worked into the soil every year. Whatever it was, from June through October the fruit just kept coming. He loved passing out lunch bags filled with ripe tomatoes to his neighbors and they seemed to enjoy them as much as he did. *Hey, Max*, they would say, *how are those tomatoes coming?* One neighbor, the house just across the street, would turn the ripe fruit into salsa and share several jars every season.

Today he was busy nipping and pruning and staking his thriving plants. It was late May and soon the blossoms would turn into small green globes, and if left unsupported, the weight would be too much for the vines to bear. The sun was nearly down on this warm May day and he started to think about the cold beer waiting for him in the fridge. His daughter and granddaughter were at the movies and they wouldn't be home until well after dark. He'd be on his own for dinner tonight.

Max had lived in the little wood frame house in a northern suburb of Sacramento for thirty years. He and his wife Stella poured lots of love and care into the place, even as the neighborhood began to decline. When Stella lost her battle with cancer eight years ago, he carried on, even though the house was empty without her. Then his daughter Marnie went through a divorce, and five years ago, Marnie and his granddaughter Jessica moved in to fill a part of the gaping hole in his life. Now all that love and care flowed in their direction.

He was gathering his tools when he heard two sharp cracks and the faint sound of glass breaking. Then two more cracks. Max was a hunter and Vietnam veteran; he knew it was gunfire. He dropped his tools and hurried to the gate at the side of the house. As he reached for the latch, he looked through the gate, and then froze.

A young man wearing a hooded sweatshirt crossed the street, headed toward a car parked at the curb, a gun in his right hand down at his side. Max could see his face clearly. He knew this boy: a neighborhood tough named Sonny. Years earlier, he had played on a Little League team Max had coached. Sonny was a handful then, difficult to control, impossible to teach, an all-around nasty little kid. And now he'd graduated to firearms. The young man climbed into the car and the wheels screeched as it tore away from the curb.

Max left the gate and backtracked to his patio. He kicked off his shoes as he entered the house and hurried to the front room. The drapes were open and through the large window he saw the house across the street and four round holes—the four shots he'd heard—in the living room window. Now he heard screams and shouts emanating from the home.

The screams and shouts continued and neighbors along the block came out on their porches to see what was happening. Sirens pierced the gathering dusk. Something tragic was unfolding and Max was a terrified witness.

<hr/>

The neighborhood swarmed with law enforcement. A half-dozen patrol cars clogged the street and yellow crime scene tape stretched along the perimeter of the lot across the way. Uniformed and plain-clothes officers moved about. Down the block, behind a set of barricades, television trucks and their crews stood by. Max sat in his La-Z-Boy recliner against the back wall of his living room. The house was dark. No one looking in the window could see him sitting there.

Okay, now what? Should Max simply walk out there and tell the deputies what he had seen? And if he did, what then? His home and family would become the next targets. It would be like hanging a bulls-eye on his front room window: shoot here. His cell phone rang, startling him so that he jumped in the chair. It was his daughter Marnie.

"Dad, what's going on? We can't get into the neighborhood. There's a line of cars here on Maple Street and I see a sheriff's roadblock up ahead."

"There was a shooting—"

"A what?"

"A shooting. Across the street at the Preston's house."

"Oh my God! Was anyone hurt?"

"I don't know yet. Look, don't come home. Don't even try to get in here. Take Jessica and go to Aunt Millie's."

"But we don't have any clothes or—"

"It's not safe here, Marnie." He could not hide the tremor in his voice. "Go to Aunt Millie's. I'll pack a bag and get some things to you tomorrow."

"But, Dad—"

Max stifled her protests and ended the call.

The activity out on the street continued and Max wondered what had happened and why. The Prestons were good neighbors, never a problem. Their little girl, Ellie, was ten years old, the same age as his granddaughter. The two girls played together constantly, walked to school together, shared birthdays. Ellie was a sweet and friendly child, round-faced and chubby, always smiling. She's the one who delivered the fresh salsa the Prestons made from his tomatoes, and she helped her mother bake cookies for the Silvers at holiday time. Ellie had an older brother—Max couldn't remember his name. Was he the target? Gangs and drugs were a reality in the neighborhood. Could it be gangbangers in some kind of turf battle? If so, Max was not getting involved. Let them go right ahead and thin out the herd.

His hands shook as he called his sister's number. Before he could tell her that Marnie and Jessica were on their way, she interrupted him.

"Max, are you watching the news?"

"What? No. No I'm not—"

"There's a report about a shooting in your neighborhood. My God, Max, someone shot a little girl."

"What?"

"A ten year old girl, Max. Someone shot her in the back of the head while she was sitting on the couch watching television. She's dead."

Millie continued, recapping the news report. Max could hardly breathe. *Oh my God! Ellie? They shot Ellie! Oh God. The animals, the goddamn animals. A little girl…a sweet innocent little girl.*

Max ended the call with Millie after making her promise to keep Marnie and Jessica safe. He would bring clothes and toothbrushes and whatever they needed tomorrow. As he put down the phone, that telltale taste rose in the back of his mouth. He hurried to the bathroom to toss the contents of his stomach, though all he could produce was bile. He rinsed his mouth and splashed water in his face. His friends often told him he resembled the actor Charles Bronson. When he looked in the mirror now, he saw a frightened old man.

———

Max parked near the phone booth adjacent to the convenience store. He turned the business card over and over in his hand. The detective had handed it to him that morning at the close of the conversation at Max's front door. No, he had seen nothing, heard nothing. He'd been in his garden out back. No, no one else was home at the time. His daughter and granddaughter had been away at a movie.

All the while, Max scanned the street behind the officer. Who was watching, timing the length of the conversation? *Just give me your damn card and get off my porch!* That's what he wanted to say. And then the detective was gone, the door closed with Max leaning hard against it, his heart racing.

Now here he was, ready to call from a payphone, certainly not from his cell that could be easily traced. He punched in the number and listened to it ring, again and again. An operator answered and he asked for Detective Roy Combs. She patched him through to Combs's mobile number.

"Hello, this is Detective Combs. Hello?"

Max held a folded handkerchief over the mouthpiece. "Yeah, I may have—" He stopped and began again. "I *have* information about the shooting on Chestnut Lane."

"Okay, let me get my notebook. Now, sir, what is your name?"

"Before I say anything, I need to know…can you protect my family, my home? You've seen what these animals will do."

"Sir, I can't promise anything until you tell me what you know."

Max slammed the phone into its cradle, then picked it up and slammed it again and again. *Sonofabitch, sonofabitch! They can't protect you, they won't protect you.* He climbed back into his car and drove around aimlessly, looking for a way out, but there were no options. Max had to tell Combs what he saw, who he saw leaving the scene with a gun in his hand. He couldn't let Sonny get away with it. He pulled into a service station and parked near a phone booth. Again, the operator patched him through.

"Detective Combs speaking. Who is calling, please?"

"Look, just tell me you'll *try* to protect my family. That's all I'm asking."

"Okay, sir, this is Mr. Silver, right? Max Silver? You live across the street from the Prestons. I spoke to you this morning. I recognize your voice, Mr. Silver."

Max's heart pounded out of his chest again. He started to hang up, but what good would that do? "Is there somewhere we can meet? Not at my house. Not in the neighborhood."

They settled on a small café a few blocks away. Max hung up the phone and then used the handkerchief to wipe the sweat from his forehead. He would tell Combs what he knew, what he saw. But he would not testify in open court, if it came to that. No way in hell would he testify.

———

Sonny had been easy to find, along with the two bangers who'd been with him that night. The three of them were being held without bail pending trial. It turned out Sonny had confessed, which was good news for Max. Roy Combs assured him he would not have to testify. They had the confession, they had the murder weapon, and the District Attorney was planning to seek the death penalty. Ellie was dead; no way to change that fact. Even though the death penalty was a joke in California, at least her killer and his pals would be going away for a long time. Max hoped to see life return to normal—or near-normal—on Chestnut Lane.

So why did Combs want to meet with him now? Were there new developments in the case?

Max walked into Gordy's Club, a working-class bar not far from the office building where he'd reported to work for thirty years. He took a seat at the bar, ordered a beer, and waited for Combs to arrive. It was mid-afternoon and the place was nearly empty. He didn't expect to see anyone he knew, not until after quitting time.

Roy Combs walked in and stood near the door, waiting for his eyes to adjust to the dim light. He was about six feet tall with a solid build. He wore rumpled slacks and a short sleeved shirt that revealed powerful forearms. His hair was cut high and tight, military style, and his expression was that of a pissed-off football coach. He saw Max and nodded toward a booth against the wall. The men shook hands, exchanged some awkward small-talk, and then Max got down to business.

"So, what's up, Roy?"

"Okay, here's the deal, Max. We are gonna need you to testify."

"What? You're shitting me. I told you I won't do that. You want me to get my family killed?"

"We don't have any choice. The judge threw out Sonny's confession."

"How the hell did that happen?"

"Sonny's got some young hotshot lawyer. They claimed the confession was coerced. The judge ruled in their favor. It's out."

"Wait a minute...you video tape those things, don't you? You have it all on tape."

Combs looked away, agitated. "We don't have a tape. The camera malfunctioned."

"Malfunctioned? Malfunctioned my ass! What did you do, Roy? You didn't tape it. You didn't even try—"

"Let it go, Max—"

"You beat it out of him!"

Combs glared at Max, eyes blazing. "That little motherfucker spit in my face! Spit in my face, Max, and called me a faggot. You're damn right I beat it out of him."

"And this is what I fought for in that rotten, stinking Vietnam? Life, liberty, the Constitution, the American Way? So that you can beat confessions out of gangbangers?"

"Don't throw the Constitution at me, old man. I served in

Desert Storm. I put my life on the line against Saddam's Elite Guard. Don't play 'holier than thou' with me."

The bartender called in their direction, telling them to keep it down or take it outside. They glared at each other, both of them breathing hard, their fists clenched on the table. Combs broke the silence.

"Look, we've still got the gun. And we've got your testimony. The DA says he can get a conviction." He paused for few seconds. "One more thing…with the confession thrown out, they set bail. Sonny and the other two are out on the street."

Max felt sick, as though he could vomit his beer right there on the table. He wanted to break the longneck bottle over Combs's head. "And what if I won't testify?"

"Come on, Max. We have your statement. We can subpoena you, treat you as a hostile witness, force you to tell the truth. Or go to jail for perjury."

Max had no way of knowing if this was true. He stared at Combs for a long time. "You knew this all along, didn't you? That you'd force me to testify. You lying bastard! And how long before Sonny finds out that I'm a witness?"

"I don't know. It's in the DA's hands. It's called discovery. They have to let the defense know all the evidence against him."

"And what will you do to protect my family?"

"We'll do what we can, increase patrols in your neighborhood—"

"Increase patrols? That's it? That's all you got?"

"Hey, it's all we can afford. Our budget is cut to the bone—"

Max bolted out of the booth and headed for the door and the parking lot. He sat in his car for a long time, his head resting on the steering wheel, fighting for composure. He was still there when Roy Combs left the bar.

It was the same dream, over and over again, through all the

years since Vietnam. Max stood on a muddy jungle road and watched the flamethrower reach out and ignite a hut. The flames leapt into the sky, black smoke billowed upward, one hut after another. Women and children streamed down the road, carrying a few meager possessions, the children crying, the women wailing. No men. Where were the men? All dead, fuel for the inferno? Or in the jungle, watching, waiting?

This is what it had come to in a country where you couldn't separate the friendlies from the hostiles, where the guy next to you died at the hands of a child with an assault rifle, where you looked into the eyes of the people you were fighting for and saw that sick, twisted mixture of fear and hatred. Why? Because you were destroying their country with napalm and agent orange and carpet bombs and your flamethrowers from hell.

The same dream, over and over, until tonight. Tonight one of the children on the road turned toward him and held out a plate of cookies. It was Ellie.

Max usually jolted awake from this dream drenched in sweat, his breath coming in great gasps. But tonight was different. Tonight he could only lie there and cry. He was awake for a long time then, trying to push the images and the questions out of his mind. How could he answer for the things he had done, and how was he different from Sonny? Who was that brilliant general who said, "Unfortunately, we had to destroy the village in order to save it"? And how many villages had they *saved*? He refused to remember; he would not count them. And so the dream would come again and again.

The District Attorney's office called to let Max know the trial date had been set. Jury selection would begin in two weeks. They would meet beforehand to go over his testimony and prepare him for cross examination. It had taken sixteen months to reach this point, the wheels of justice grinding away, slow but relentless.

Max was ready, at least as ready as he could be, and he felt an eerie calm now that decisions had been made and set in motion. His daughter and granddaughter were settled with family in Minnesota, two thousand miles away. His house was nearly empty, everything he owned donated or sold on this thing his daughter showed him called Craig's List. There were a few pots, pans, and utensils in the kitchen, his meager wardrobe in the bedroom closet, his recliner in the living room, along with a framed portrait of Stella on the fireplace mantle. His footsteps echoed as he walked through the house.

He filled his days with routine. Two mornings a week, he attended minyan at the synagogue where he'd been a member since the mid-seventies, and he observed yahrzeit and attended services to say Kaddish for his parents and for Stella. He read voraciously, went to lunch at favorite cafés, and stopped by Gordy's for a cold beer or two. And of course there was his beloved garden. This year's crop of tomatoes had been exceptional, even by Max's standards. He'd given away so many that he was sure the neighbors were sick of tomatoes. Some of the rest he'd turned into soup and stocked his freezer with plastic containers filled with the red-orange liquid.

He had sold his bed, and now he slept in the La-Z-Boy. Among the stack of books next to his chair was Stella's dog-eared volume of *Tanakh –The Holy Scriptures*. In *Deuteronomy 25:19*, he had underlined these words: "...you shall blot out the memory of Amalek from under the heaven. Do not forget it!" And in *I Samuel 15:3*: "Now go and smite Amalek, and utterly destroy all that they have, and spare them not..." Amalek, who attacked from the rear, plundered the sick and the weak, and murdered women and children.

Max would not forget.

Propped against the wall, just behind the chair, was his

Winchester 11-87. The twelve-gauge shotgun was a relic of his days as an avid duck and pheasant hunter. Max had given up the sport when most of his hunting buddies either died or moved away. Now the well-maintained 11-87 stood loaded and ready, one shell in the chamber, four in the magazine. With the trial date set, he was sure they were coming for him.

———~w~o~o~e~o~o~e~o~o~o~w~———

The night they came, Max was wide awake. Since the call from the DA's office, he'd developed the habit of setting an alarm for a little after 2:00 a.m. when the bars closed, figuring they would get a load on before heading his way.

The old black Honda Civic with the faded paint job and bright chrome wheels rolled slowly past the house, circled the block and rolled by again. Car doors slammed, Max's signal. He turned the recliner sideways and positioned himself behind it, one knee on the floor, the shotgun resting on the arm of the chair.

Two figures walked across his front lawn, up to the low shrubs that grew in front of the living room window. One of them carried a heavy tool with a long handle. They peered in through the window, and then, unable to see anything or anyone, they went to the front porch. A sledgehammer blasted the wooden door frame to pieces, splitting the stillness. The door swung open and the two men moved into the room.

"Oh, Maxie...old ma-an...where are you?" The man in the lead called out in a sing-song voice. The one behind him laughed softly.

Max squeezed the trigger and the shotgun blast rocked the room. The first man flew back against the wall and crumpled to the floor. A new shell was in the chamber and Max pulled the trigger again. He saw a series of muzzle flashes and braced for the shock and burn of the bullets heading his way. The shock and burn never happened. The slugs slammed into the wall behind him. Both men were down on the floor, moving, but just barely. Max stood up and walked the few steps across the room. The second one through the door, the one who had returned fire, was Sonny—Amalek himself.

Max waited, the shotgun ready. Would someone from the Civic come running to provide backup? But then came the sound of the engine racing as the car sped away. He looked at the bloody mess on the wall and at his feet. Should he fire one more shell into the chest of each man? No need. They were no longer moving.

Max placed the shotgun on the recliner and went through the kitchen and into the garage. He retrieved a five-gallon can and brought it into the house. He would douse the bodies and the walls with gasoline until the can was empty, then stand back and toss a match into the room. The little wood frame house would be *saved*, just like all those huts and all those villages in Vietnam.

Instead he stood motionless, staring at Stella's portrait on the mantle, tears clouding his eyes.

He set the can on the floor, pulled his cell phone from his pocket and dialed 911. The dispatcher led him through a series of questions, confirming his name and address, and the fact that two men had been shot while breaking into his home.

"I'm sending the sheriff and an ambulance, Mr. Silver."

The ambulance wasn't necessary but he didn't argue. "Okay... and you should notify Sheriff's Detective Roy Combs. This is his case."

Max traced the bullet holes in the wall with his finger as he spoke to the woman on the phone. He thought about Minnesota and his daughter and granddaughter. He could not wait to be with them. Several questions played in his mind. It was late September now: were the leaves there starting to turn color? Would they need to purchase new clothes for the Minnesota winter? And what varieties of tomato grew there?

Sirens grew ever louder as the call ended.

Note: Elvira Campos of North Highlands, California, was shot and killed as she sat in the front room of her home on May 18, 2013. She was ten years old. This tale of vengeance is for her.

ONE PERFECT DAY

from *Monday Update*

Jason loved the Tower Café, especially the patio perched like an island at the corner of Broadway and Land Park Drive. He could sit there in the shade on all but the hottest Sacramento days, or bundled in a jacket and scarf in the heart of winter, and feel completely at home. Along the edge of the walk on the east side, palm trees provided the first layer of protection, then ancient ferns that had been pruned over the years to behave like small trees, and finally twisted old cypress and a few Japanese maples forming the inner ring. The tabletops were old redwood, lacquered to a high polish, and the bench seats that lined the perimeter were made of the same wood. A bowl of soup, a half-loaf of bread, and a good glass of wine were all it took to make it the best place in town.

Lauren was late, but that was her usual pattern. She was always too busy, never enough hours in the day. He sipped his wine and waited, enjoying the sunny June day and the lunchtime crowd, eavesdropping on the couple sitting next to him as they whispered intimate secrets.

Then Jason saw her, coming from the parking lot past the theater entrance and around the walk that led to the café. She was wearing a sleeveless blouse, khaki shorts and sandals and, as usual, she looked wonderful. He waved to her and caught her eye and she smiled and waved back.

What would she say when he asked the question?

Lauren made her way to the table with her trademark stride: strong, purposeful, confident, not at all ladylike. Among other things, she was a fine athlete. You only had to watch her walk to know that. He rose and moved out from behind the table to give her a welcoming hug and a kiss on the cheek. He recognized the smell of her shampoo as he held her, perhaps a beat too long. It had been a long time, too long, and he realized in that moment how much he missed her.

"Thanks for coming, Lauren. God, you look wonderful. I've missed you."

She looked at him for a moment, and then a smile broke across her face. "I've missed you too, Jason. I shouldn't say it—but what the hell—it's true."

He flagged down their waiter to order a glass of wine for her and they chatted amiably, getting caught up on the latest events in their lives. Lauren was an attorney on a partnership track with a local firm that lobbied the state legislature on behalf of various business clients. She was very good at her job and she knew it. It was obvious in the way she carried herself and the confidence she brought to any topic you cared to discuss. To Jason, she had it all: beauty, brains, *chutzpah*, and one of the prettiest golf swings he'd ever seen. He listened as she ran down the gist of a particular piece of legislation she was currently championing and he wondered why he'd let her get away. Of course, he knew the answers and could tick them off like talking points. He was in his fifties; she was barely thirty. She dreamed of raising a family; he was beyond that point in his life. He was raised Catholic; she was Jewish. There were other reasons, but those were the big three. And yet, he'd never been happier than when they were together. He should never have let her go, but he was glad now that he had.

They ordered salads and another glass of wine as the conversation rolled on. Jason knew where the conversation was going and he was ready to answer honestly. He was hoping that the crowd around them would be thinned out when the time came.

The salads were delivered and they dug in with gusto. Jason loved the way she attacked her food. There wasn't an ounce of dainty in this amazing woman. She was strong, confident, and direct.

"So, Jason, enough chit chat. How are you? And why did you ask me to meet you? And no bullshit. Please."

"Okay, Lauren." He took a deep breath. "It's back. It has spread. There's nothing more they can do. I don't have much time, maybe six months at the most."

Lauren's eyes welled and her lower lip trembled as she reached for his hand. He went on then, telling her of his plan to return to New Orleans, to be with his extended family there. His sister had agreed to take him in and make him comfortable; they had always been close and he was sure this was the right thing to do. And then he told Lauren of his dream of a perfect day—just one perfect day—that he would like to spend with her. And soon, while he was still strong, before he had to pack up and leave town. He knew it was a lot to ask, certainly more than he deserved, but would she at least think about it?

Lauren stared at him for a long time, dabbed her eyes with the napkin, dropped it on what remained of her salad, stood and walked away. Jason didn't try to stop her. He wasn't the least bit surprised; in fact, he'd kind of expected this reaction. He leaned back against the bench seat and sipped his wine until the glass was empty.

He was on his way to the parking lot when his cell phone rang. "Hello."

"Okay, I'll do it." She was trying hard not to cry. "You're a bastard to ask. You know that don't you?"

"Yes."

"Give me a few days to regroup. Then let me know when you want to do it. Okay?"

"Okay. And Lauren—"

"Yeah?"

"Thank you."

The line went dead. He put his phone back in his pocket.

———————————————

Estelle took the steaming cups of tea from the counter and placed them on the kitchen table, one in front of her daughter. There were sugar cubes and a small pitcher of milk, along with a plate of freshly baked shortbread cookies.

"Lauren, tell me again, how did this new *thing* with Jason get started?"

"He called me last week, Mom. We met for lunch, and he just asked me."

"I thought this involvement with Jason was over. I thought you were moving on."

"It is over, Mom. It really is. It's just one day."

"Oh, please. Lauren, honey, he's just dragging you back into his life."

"Mom, *it is just one day!*"

"Sure, one day here, one day there. Before you know it—"

"Mom, stop! Please. This is just something I have to do, that I want to do. And then he'll be gone, to New Orleans, to be with his sister…until the end." The words caught in her throat and she blinked her eyes.

"Darling, look what this is doing to you. You know I never saw this relationship working out. He's in a completely different place in his life. He's—what?—twenty years older than you? And a Catholic, for God's sake! How much time did you waste on this man?"

"It was not a waste, Ma. I loved him. And he loved me—"

"And then he dumped you."

"Mom, he got sick! He got sick and didn't want me to have to live with it, to be his nurse. It was a selfless thing he tried to do—"

"And now he's sick again. And now he wants you back. How selfless is that?"

"Please, please, PLEASE just stop! Or I swear I'm going to leave. I will not have this conversation with you." She could not hold back the tears now.

"Darling, look at you. *Oy gavalt!* My *shayne kop,* look what this is doing. Calm down, *mamala.* Have some tea. Have a cookie. I baked them this morning, just for you."

It was useless, a debate Lauren could never win. Without saying another word, she left the table and hurried to the bathroom to dry her eyes and repair her makeup. She stayed for a long time, staring into the sink, then into the mirror. She stayed until she was sure the crying was done.

———

Valerie was quiet for several seconds, biting her lip, biting her tongue, trying not to jump down her brother's throat. She thought he had called just to chat, to bring her up to date on his prognosis, to let her know for sure when he was coming to New Orleans. But that wasn't it. He had news, news that involved Lauren, who was not Valerie's favorite person. Finally, she couldn't hold back.

"Jason, Jason, Jason. Please tell me you're kidding."

"Look, Sis, I'm not kidding. This is something I want to do, something *we* want to do together, before I leave Sacramento for good."

"So you want to spend a day with the Jew girl—"

"Wait a minute, Val. 'Jew girl'? Where is that coming from?"

"Okay, I'm sorry. Jewish girl. It's just, well, you know I never liked her."

"And may I ask why? You met her exactly once. Or was it twice? What is it you didn't like?"

"I don't know…she just seemed so…pushy."

"Oh, so if it's a man he's confident, or aggressive. But if it's a woman, she's pushy?"

"Look, Jason, I just never thought she was right for you. I

mean, you're a practicing Catholic. You know how *they* think. If the mother is Jewish, the kids are Jewish. Case closed."

"Who said anything about kids? And anyway, this is my decision. I'm not asking for your permission. I'm sorry if that sounds harsh."

They were both quiet then. The basic truth could not be changed. Jason's condition was terminal, he was coming home to die, and what he did beforehand made little difference.

"Jason, I'm sorry. I won't mention it again. I know you have to do what's right for you. It's just…it's just that I can't help but worry about you."

"You have to trust me on this, Val. Have a little faith that I know what I'm doing. Okay?"

She was biting her lip again, but she managed to say, "Okay."

He signed his name one last time and then pushed the document across the table. Seth, Jason's attorney, picked it up, perused it briefly, and then added it to the stack he was accumulating.

"Okay, Jason. I think that's it. As the saying goes, 'your affairs are in order.'"

They were sitting on the patio outside Bella Bru on a bright and sunny day. The temperature was climbing but it was very pleasant sitting in the shade. The place was busy with the usual lunchtime crowd. Jason took a sip from the tall glass of iced tea.

"Thanks, Seth. I appreciate all the work you've done. How soon will escrow close on my condo?"

"By the end of the month, as you requested. The sale of the business will take a little longer. I'll keep you posted. Your sister is the executor of your will and she has power of attorney. She'll be well taken care of when all is said and done. As will Lauren Goodman. If you don't mind my asking, Jason, who is Lauren?"

Jason paused for a moment, not sure how much he wanted Seth to know.

"Someone I love." He said it simply, then looked away.

"Oh. Will she be with you in New Orleans?"

"No. No she will not."

"Well, I'm sure you'll miss her."

Seth's cell phone rang and vibrated, dancing on the faux stone table top. He glanced at the screen and looked up at Jason.

"I should take this call. Will you excuse me?"

"Sure, Seth. Go ahead."

Seth stood and walked away from the table, the phone pressed to his left ear, his right arm gesturing somewhat dramatically as he responded to the caller. Jason thought about the phrase *I'm sure you'll miss her.* Seth was right about that. He'd miss her for many reasons—intelligence, sense of humor, compassion, zest for living. He could go on. But he found his mind dwelling on one thing: her kisses. In all of his experience, no one could compare. Her lips were soft, her mouth a perfect fit to his. Whether just barely touching, or long and deep during lovemaking, her kisses were thrilling, moving, unforgettable. He closed his eyes and imagined her there at that moment, her lips parted, just inches away, the prelude to a perfect kiss.

"Okay, Jason. Sorry for the interruption. I think we are done here, my friend. I have to go into the office. Some pressing business that can't wait."

Jason stood to shake Seth's hand and say goodbye. He watched his attorney walk briskly toward the parking lot, clearly a man on a mission. Jason sat down at the table, took a deep breath and exhaled slowly. He went back to his meditation on the magic, the chemistry, the thrill of kissing Lauren.

———

Jason pulled the chair over in front of the large plate glass window next to the bed. The drapes were drawn wide open so that he could look out over the lights of San Francisco toward the Bay Bridge and the East Bay hills beyond. Their room was on the twenty-third floor of the Hilton and the view was spectacular. Lauren was sleeping quietly, her back turned toward him, her bare shoulder exposed. It was cool in the room and he reached out to pull the sheet and blanket over her. He knew he should be sleeping too, but it would take a while for the medication to kick in and the pain to subside. And so he sat, drinking in the view.

It had been a busy day, beginning with nine holes of golf at the venerable Haggin Oaks course in Sacramento. They'd teed-off just after sunrise, the dew still heavy on the fairways and greens. He loved watching Lauren golf and her game was as sharp as ever. She always played from the men's tees and generally outdrove him. In high school, she'd toyed with the idea of professional golf. Instead, she'd poured all that competitive drive into the law. When they'd walked off the ninth green and headed back toward the clubhouse, Jason was nine strokes over par. Lauren was two under. She was that good.

After golf, they had rushed to his condo to shower and change clothes and then hit the road to San Francisco. Tickets were waiting at the will-call window at AT&T Park for the Giants' game against the Milwaukee Brewers. A young lefty named Madison Bumgarner was starting for the Giants and Jason was looking forward to seeing him pitch. He was not disappointed. After giving up a homerun to Ryan Braun in the first inning, Bumgarner settled down and pitched a beautiful game. Brian Wilson closed out the ninth inning for the Giants' win. Lauren loved baseball almost as much as Jason did, and the defending World Champion Giants were her favorites. The 2011 season was off to a good start.

Lauren stirred in bed now, mumbling a few words in her sleep. He continued to gaze out the window, admiring the lights strung along the suspension cables of the bridge. San Francisco: city of hills, city of bridges, city of cable cars, and wonderful food. It was truly beautiful, in his mind the most beautiful city in the world, especially when viewed from afar—from the Sausalito shore on a sunny day, or from the Marin headlands, looking down on the Golden Gate. And from way up here above the city streets, with just the faintest echoes of horns and sirens from the traffic racing below.

Down on the street, it was another story. Homeless people sleeping on heating grates or camped in doorways, everything they owned piled into shopping carts, the smell of piss and vomit clogging the air. The contrasts were shocking if you let yourself think about it. Cocktails at the Top of the Mark; a bottle of Thunderbird in the Tenderloin. Tony Bennett at the Venetian Room; singing for spare change in Union Square. Bacon-wrapped swordfish at the Tadich Grill; digging through the dumpster in the alley out back. The gap between life's winners and losers grew ever wider with no solutions in sight.

After the ballgame, they'd checked into the Hilton, showered and changed, and set out in search of a memorable meal. This took them to Benihana in Japantown. They knew it was a tourist haven, but they didn't care. It had always been a favorite, watching the teppanyaki chefs do their thing with shrimp and chicken and steak, knives flashing, shrimp tails flying, lively conversation with perfect strangers gathered around the grill. They always left happy.

After dinner, it was on to a jazz club located just off Broadway to hear a quintet headed by Joshua Redman. They sat through a couple of sets and left the club amazed yet again at Redman's artistry.

Time for one more stop: the Buena Vista Café for an Irish Coffee. And then they caught the Powell & Hyde cable car back to Union Square, just a short walk from the Hilton. They had managed to cram all of Jason's favorite things into a single day.

His eyes were closing now, his head nodding. Just then, the

lights of a ship slid under the Bay Bridge, heading toward the Golden Gate and the open water beyond. *Where is she headed? What ports of call? Maybe she's bound for New Orleans, just like me.*

Lauren turned over in bed, her eyes blinked open and she smiled. "Hey. You okay?"

"Yeah, sure."

"Come make love to me again?"

"Too late, babe. Pills are kickin' in."

"Then come keep me warm."

"That, I can do."

"How was your day? Was it like you dreamed?"

Jason stood and pushed the chair aside, then leaned down to kiss her one more time.

"It was perfect," he said. "Thanks to you."

EDDIE

E ddie walked up to home plate, his eyes focused on me all the way. I stood in the third base coach's box and looked in at him—all five feet and ninety pounds—and tried to think of something I could say as his coach, something that might actually help. It was the bottom of the sixth, two outs, bases loaded, and we were down by one run.

Eddie was small for a twelve year-old. Several of his teammates towered over him and outweighed him by thirty pounds, but he was a good kid, a good teammate, always smiling, full of fun. It had been a pleasure to have him on my team. We'd had a good year, good enough to play in this post-season Tournament-of-Champions. And now here we were: our last at bat, one run to tie, two to win, or we could simply go home, the season over for another year.

I motioned for Eddie to come to me, and I met him halfway. I put my right hand on his shoulder and bent down to talk to him, mouthing the clichés that have served coaches so well since the time of Abner Doubleday.

"Okay, Eddie, just relax, take a deep breath, get a good pitch to hit, put your best swing on it. Okay? No worries. Hey it's just a game. Right? Have some fun—"

At that moment, in the middle of my inane monologue, I put my left hand on Eddie's chest. His heart was jumping into my hand—thump, thump, thump—like someone beating a bass drum. It stopped me cold.

I'd grown up playing baseball from the time I was seven years old, and I knew what the pressure was like, especially when the adults tell you it's a "big game," and your parents are in the stands, and there are hundreds of people watching, yelling, shouting your name. I knew all of that. But I'd let myself forget. That is, until Eddie's heart was in my hand. I said the only thing that came to mind.

"Hey, just give it your best. Whatever happens, it won't change the way I feel about you."

Eddie turned and headed back to the plate. I'm sure his heart rate was accelerating.

I wish I had a happy ending for you, a miracle line drive to left-center bringing in two runs for the win. But that's not what happened. Eddie struck out.

I trotted in to scoop him up and carry him the few steps to the dugout, tears beginning to well in his eyes and mine. I can't remember what I said, but I know it didn't help. Nothing would have helped.

That was twenty-five years ago. A lot of seasons have come and gone since then, for me and for Eddie. He grew a little, packed on some muscle, and became an all-conference rugby player in college. But, I would bet Eddie remembers that baseball game like it was yesterday, just as I will always remember his heart leaping into my hand.

CLOSURE

A one-act play

from *Monday Update*

C ast (in order of appearance):
   Maria, a staff member at Carlo's Restaurant
   Solomon Milton, an attorney
   Carlo Vitelli, proprietor of Carlo's
   Vincente D'Antoni, head waiter
   Joe (Giuseppe), bartender
   Mario, pianist/vocalist

The Scene:
The interior of Carlo's, an upscale restaurant situated in a suburban shopping center in Sacramento, California. A waiting area and coat check room are at stage right, just inside the front door. The bar is on the right, separated from the dining area by a low partition. The walls of the dining room are weathered brick and the floor is covered in a dark, patterned carpet. In the back corner to the left is a piano bar, built in a horseshoe that wraps around a baby grand set on a riser. The banquettes around the perimeter are well-maintained maroon leather. The tables in mid-room are large with comfortable chairs covered in the same leather. The lighting is dim, primarily sconces mounted on the walls and recessed lighting in the ceiling above the tables. On the walls, highlighted by the sconces, are large

framed oil paintings picturing Tuscan country scenes. The tables are covered with sparkling white table cloths and set with sterling silver tableware and maroon napkins. The atmosphere is quiet, sophisticated, reminiscent of special occasions, memorable food, drink, and entertainment.

[As the scene opens, staff members are busy preparing the restaurant for the evening dinner trade, even though the doors will not open for another two hours. People hurry about placing fresh flowers in small vases on each table, arranging and rearranging the table settings, touching up the carpet with a manual carpet sweeper. A man sits at the piano, noodling around the keyboard, rehearsing a song to add to his playlist. His voice, a well-worn baritone that speaks of whiskey and cigarettes, is heard above the hustle and bustle:]

> *I keep goin' back to Joe's*
> *To that table in the corner*
> *Sippin' wine and starin' at the door...*

The singer pauses as Maria, a young staff member, leads a man to a table at center stage. He is of medium height and build, balding, wearing a well-tailored suit, highly polished oxfords, and carrying an expensive leather briefcase.]

MARIA: Pease have a seat, Mr. Milton. *[She pulls a chair out from the table.]* I'll tell Mr. Vitelli that you are here.

[The piano player resumes his explorations, pausing now and then to make notes on his sheet music. His playing—refining a personal arrangement of "I Keep Going Back to Joe's"—continues intermittently throughout the scene.]

SOL: Thank you.

[He places his briefcase on the table and sits, rather uncomfortably, looking around the room. The restaurant owner enters from stage right and approaches the table. He is a courtly and formal man, in his early sixties, with a full head of gray hair and a thin salt-and-pepper moustache. Sol stands to greet him.]

CARLO *[speaking with a slight Italian accent]*: Mr. Milton? I am Carlo Vitelli. It is so nice of you to come.

[They clasp hands firmly, holding eye contact for several seconds.]

SOL: Please call me Sol. It is a pleasure to meet you, Mr. Vitelli. I've enjoyed many a fine meal here in your beautiful establishment.

CARLO: Thank you…that is good to know. Please, can I get you anything? Perhaps a cappuccino?

SOL: No, thanks, I'm fine. I appreciate your willingness to meet with me, Mr. Vitelli.

[He opens his briefcase and hands Carlo his card.]

CARLO: Of course.

SOL: As you know, I represent Mr. Richard Carter in all matters. Not only is he my client, Rick has been my friend since our grammar school days. He asked me to come here today to offer his sincere apology for the incident that took place here last night. He wanted me to give you this.
[He hands an envelope to Carlo who just stares at it.] Please…go ahead…open it.

[Carlo opens the envelope and removes a single sheet of note paper. Folded inside the paper are several hundred dollar bills. He reads the note and a wry smile crosses his face.]

CARLO: It is an apology. Mr. Carter has offered to pay for any damage, and he asks that this money be shared among the staff. He really didn't need to do that.

SOL: Well, he is a little embarrassed and he just wants to make amends. Now…you may be wondering why I asked to speak to you.

CARLO: As a matter of fact, yes, I was.

SOL: As you may already know, Rick has declined to file a complaint over the incident. But in his best interests, I feel that I need to learn as many of the facts as possible, should any legal questions arise.

CARLO: Of course, I understand completely. How is Rick? Is he going to be all right?

SOL: Well, I'm afraid his jaw may be broken. It is quite swollen and he is in a bit of pain. I've finally convinced him to see a doctor, although he resisted. He has an appointment tomorrow morning.

CARLO: Please send him my regards…as well as from the entire staff. He is a favorite here at Carlo's, as you already know.

SOL: I'll be sure to let him know of your concern. Now…I'm sure you are pressed for time, but it would be most helpful if you could take a few minutes to tell me what happened last night…from your point of view, of course.

CARLO: Of course, but perhaps I should give you a little of the…uh…background.

SOL: That would be fine. Oh, and if you don't mind, I'd like to take a few notes. I just can't trust my memory. *[He laughs and takes a pen and legal pad from his briefcase and places them on the table.]*

CARLO *[leaning in]*: Let's see now…how to begin. About two years ago, early '72 if my memory serves me, Rick met Allison right here at Carlo's, sitting at the piano bar. She was here with friends, celebrating a birthday, and they struck up a conversation. I could see the sparks fly immediately, even though she was younger—perhaps ten or twelve years his junior. He seemed quite taken with her, and who could blame him? She is a lovely girl and they seemed to enjoy each other's company, talking and laughing, even singing along with Mario.

SOL: Mario?

CARLO: Yes, our man at the piano bar. Anyway, it seems that Rick and Allison quickly became…an…

SOL: An item?

CARLO: Yes, that is a good word for it. It was obvious that he adored her. They would sit, holding hands, talking, laughing, staring into each other's eyes. Even at my age, I found it inspiring. They were a lovely couple. And so it went, through all of the months, right up until…*[trails off]*

SOL: Until when?

CARLO: Until February of this year. Rick called to make a reservation for Valentine's Day. I spoke to him personally. He said he planned to pop the question, to propose marriage, right here in their favorite booth. Of course, we made all the arrangements to help make it a special occasion. The chef was ready to prepare their favorite chocolate soufflé, a special bottle of Champagne was in the cooler, our head waiter, Vincente, was assigned to their table, Mario was prepared to play their favorite songs. Carlo's was in a high state of readiness. *[He pauses dramatically, remembering.]*

SOL: So…what happened next?

[Maria approaches the table and whispers a message in Carlo's ear.]

CARLO: Please excuse me for a few minutes. I have an issue to resolve with one of our suppliers. In the meantime, let me send Vincente to you. I am sure he can continue the story.

[Carlo leaves the table as Sol scribbles his notes. The piano player continues working on his arrangement:

> *Joe keeps busy at the bar*
> *Never asks me where you are*
> *He was there when you walked out on me…*

A tall, lean man with graying hair, possibly in his fifties, approaches the table. He is dressed in pressed black slacks, a starched white shirt and black tie, with a spotless white apron tied around his waist. He is as formal and courtly as his boss, but with a definite flair for the dramatic.]

VINCENTE: Mr. Milton? Allow me to introduce myself. I am Vincente D'Antoni, head waiter. *[Vincente bows slightly, and then extends his hand.]* How may I be of assistance?

SOL: A pleasure to meet you, Vincente. Please, have a seat. *[Vincente sits opposite Sol.]* Carlo was taking me through the story of Mr. Carter and Miss Allison. We were up to the evening of this past Valentine's Day.

VINCENTE: Ah, yes. Valentine's Day. Always a wonderful occasion at Carlo's, the place filled with lovers of all ages. Perhaps my favorite of all the days of the year.

SOL *[anxious to move the story along]*: And Rick and Allison were here, at your table?

VINCENTE: Yes, yes...I had cleared away their dinner dishes and we knew the proposal was imminent. The kitchen was hard at work on the soufflé, and I was bringing the Champagne when I saw Mr. Rick reach into his jacket pocket and place the ring box in front of her. *[He pauses, recalling the moment.]*

SOL: And then?

VINCENTE: And then disaster! Calamity! Miss Allison opened the box, looked at the ring, looked at Mr. Rick, and said "I can't do this!" She slid out of the booth and ran for the front door. She didn't even stop for her coat.

SOL: And Rick? What did he do?

VINCENTE: He sat there stunned...for several seconds. I stood near the table, frozen, unsure of what to do or say, holding the Champagne like an idiot. Finally, he looked up at me and said, "Vincente, please bring the check. Cancel the soufflé. And we won't be needing the Champagne." In all my experience as a waiter, I'd never been so sad for anyone.

SOL [shaking his head sadly]: I can imagine.

VINCENTE: After that, Mr. Rick would come in several nights a week, sitting in that booth, drinking, sometimes to excess, staring at the door. After a few weeks, he wouldn't even sit in the booth. He would occupy a stool at the piano bar, listening to Mario, still with his eyes on the door, as though he expected her to walk in at any moment. I must tell you, Mr. Milton, I've never seen a man so utterly devastated.

[Carlo returns to the table, obviously in a hurry.]

CARLO: Excuse me, Mr. Milton, but I must take Vincente away for a few minutes. Perhaps you'd like to speak to Giuseppe at the bar, or Mario at the piano? They were both here last night.

SOL: Certainly, that would be fine.

[With that Carlo and Vincente hurry away. Sol picks up his note pad and walks over to the bar.]

GIUSEPPE: Hello, counselor. Yeah, the word spreads fast. I hear you represent Rick Carter. Damn, what a disaster that was! [laughs] Can I get you anything?

SOL: No thanks, I'm good. I just want to ask you a couple of questions...[skeptically] Giuseppe is it?

GIUSEPPE [laughing]: Actually, my name is Joe...Joe O'Connor. Carlo likes everyone to have an Italian name. Something about creating ambience. [laughs again] And you would be?

SOL: Sol Milton. And yes, I represent Rick Carter. I'm here gathering information about last night's incident.

JOE: Incident? Yeah, it sure as hell was. *[He is busy shaking a drink. He places a chilled long-stem martini glass on the bar in front of Sol and pours it half full from the shaker.]* There…try that and tell me what you think.

SOL *[taking a sip of the drink]*: Hmmm…very good, but a little sweet for my taste.

JOE: Yeah…me too. It's an apple martini. Or an appletini. Some cute little name like that. Ya know, it used to be that a guy only needed to know five basic drinks to get by: A Bloody Mary, an Old Fashion, a Martini, a Manhattan, and…and…damn, can't remember number five. Anyway, now-a-days it's a free-for-all. They come in asking for new drinks every night, like it's a game of stump-the-barkeep. It's all I can do to keep up. *[He laughs as Sol takes another sip.]* So, counselor, you want to know about last night?

SOL: Yeah, Joe. Tell me what you know.

JOE: Well…first let me tell you something…Rick is a good guy and you know what they say about good guys finishing last. He deserved better treatment than he got from Allison, that little gold digger. So what I'm sayin' here is that it's kinda hard for me to be impartial.

SOL: I understand. Just tell me what you saw.

JOE: I only saw the end of it. Rick was sitting in the booth over there in the corner with Allison and Johnny—that's Allison's new fella, or should I say victim?—and I heard voices getting loud and out of control, and then the two guys stood up, nose to nose. Then Johnny stepped back and threw a short right hand flush on Rick's left cheek. Rick went down like a sack of potatoes. He grabbed the tablecloth as he was goin' down and pulled the table full of dishes with him. The racket was terrific. All hell broke loose…several dames in the crowd screamed.

SOL: Then what?

JOE: Johnny threw some money down on the table and he and Allison scrammed outta here.

SOL: Do you have any idea what precipitated it?

JOE: Huh?

SOL: Do you know what caused the fight? Did you hear what was said?

JOE: Nah, too far away. But Vincente was right there. I'm sure he could tell you. You know… *[Joe pauses for several seconds]* over the last few weeks, Rick would sit at the bar when I wasn't too busy and talk about what happened on Valentine's Day. He told me all he really wanted was closure. He just wanted to know why. Why did she walk out on him back in February when he proposed? Closure. It's a funny word, isn't it? Anyway, that's all he wanted. *[Joe pauses again as Sol takes another sip of the appletini.]* So, that's about it, Mr. Milton.

SOL *[finishing his notes]*: Thanks for the drink, Joe. I think I'll spend a couple of minutes with Mario.

[Sol walks from the bar area over to the piano bar and takes a seat on the stool closest to Mario who is busy rehearsing another verse.

> *Now I pray you'll walk back in*
> *Sayin' look what fools we've been*

Then we'll celebrate a happy new beginning...

Mario smiles and greets him with his whiskey growl.]

MARIO: I knew you'd get around to me sooner or later. I know you're here about Rick and the little dust-up last night. How is he doin'?

SOL: It could be a broken jaw. We'll find out tomorrow.

MARIO: Ah, that's a shame...he's one of the good guys. You know, we do a thing for our best customers. When they walk into the dining room, I play their favorite song. For Rick, I would do "Take the A-Train." He loves Ellington! *[He plays the familiar intro and goes into the first verse.]* As for Allison, well, she loves *West Side Story*. The minute Carlo would bring her into the room, I'd play "I Feel Pretty." *[He plays a fragment.]* She would beam that smile from ear to ear and blow me a kiss. What a girl! It was sad when she walked out on him Valentine's night, what I call the Valentine's Day Massacre. *[He plays a few notes of something dramatic.]*

SOL *[smiles]*: Tell me, Mario, what did you see last night?

MARIO: Probably the same thing Joe told you. I heard voices rising, every head in the place turned in their direction, then Rick and the other guy jumped up face to face. Rick said one more thing, one last remark that broke the camel's back, and the guy popped him. What a mess! Rick pulled the whole table down with him. Ladies screaming, guys shouting. I started playing "The Star Spangled Banner." It's an old trick to restore order when emotions are running high. Sure enough, everybody looked at me like I was crazy and it got real quiet. And then Allison and her guy were gone.

SOL: Anything else you can tell me?

MARIO: Yeah, well…I really can't blame Rick. He was sitting here with me, mindin' his own business, when Allison came in. Carlo brought her in to the table alone—I guess her date was parking the car or something—and I automatically starting playing "I Feel Pretty." She smiled and looked this way and saw Rick sitting here, and her face froze. And then Johnny—I think that's his name—walks in. *[He laughs.]* I shoulda played "Send in the Clowns." *[He plays a few bars.]* Anyway, there they are, sitting in Rick and Allison's old booth, and Rick sitting here trying to contain himself. I honestly think Rick would have gotten up and left, I really do. Actually, I think he was about to do just that when this guy, Johnny, gets up and comes over. He asks Rick to join them. I guess he was just trying to be a nice guy…you know, the bigger man, and all that. Rick should have headed for the door, but instead he doubles down and accepts the offer. After that, I it was just a matter of time.

SOL: Did you hear what set it off?

MARIO: Nope…too busy entertaining my fans, know what I mean? But you should talk to Vincente. He can tell you. *[He plays a few dramatic chords and then pauses.]* You know, it's a funny thing…I know Rick saw the punch coming…I mean the guy stepped back and wound up, for God's sake…but he never made a move to protect himself. Strange, don't you think?

SOL: Yeah, very strange. *[He gets up to leave.]* Thanks, Mario. Much appreciated.

MARIO: Hey, I'm here five nights a week. Come on by anytime. There's always room at the bar…and in my jar.

[Mario nods toward the large fishbowl on the bar. Sol takes out his wallet, drops in a five dollar bill, and then moves back to the original table. He catches Vincente's eye as he moves through the room and motions for him to come over. The two men sit down at the table. Mario begins to noodle around the keyboard again, working on his arrangement.]

SOL: Vincente, you were standing near the table when the incident took place. Can you tell me what happened? What set it off?

VINCENTE *[his face suddenly flushed]*: Well...yes...though it is very embarrassing...certain words I don't care to repeat.

SOL: This stays between you and me. Just tell me what you heard.

VINCENTE: Yes, well...they were just conversing, just general small talk over the appetizers, and Mr. Rick said, "Tell me, how did you two get together?" And Mr. Johnny said they met in the office where they both work, and that they'd had a few casual dates, but it was the week before Valentine's Day when they took a trip together to San Francisco, a wonderful, romantic weekend in The City, and they realized they were falling in love. *[He pauses, reluctant to continue.]*

SOL: And?

VINCENTE: I can only guess...but I think Mr. Rick realized that this trip, this romantic weekend, was just before he proposed marriage to Miss Allison. She was already seeing Mr. Johnny.

SOL: What then?

VINCENTE: Then the fuse was lit. Mr. Rick began to say mean things, hurtful things, intimate sexual things about Miss

Allison—does she still do this…does she still like that. It became more and more hurtful and ugly as he went along. And she and Mr. Johnny kept telling him to calm down, to stop, please stop, to shut up, before he went too far. But it was too late. The two men stood up and Mr. Rick made one more ugly remark about Miss Allison—and Mr. Johnny punched him in the jaw. And then Mr. Rick was on the floor with broken plates and glassware all around him. It was terrible. The worst I've ever seen. *[His voice trails away.]*

[While Vincente is recounting the events, Carlo rejoins them at the table. He is there nodding quietly as Vincente finishes his story.]

CARLO: I came over quickly when I saw Rick on the floor. I knelt by him, along with Vincente, to see how badly he was hurt. I called to the bar for a towel with ice. I pressed the cold towel to his jaw and I asked him, "Are you okay? Should we call an ambulance?" "No!" he said. "Should we call the police?" "No!" he said again, and then he mumbled one more thing that I did not catch. Vincente and I helped him up and into my office where he sat for thirty minutes or so.

SOL: And then?

CARLO: And then I drove him home.

SOL *[finishing his notes]*: I think I have everything I need. *[He places the note pad and pen in his briefcase and closes it.]* Carlo, thank you for your time and for making your staff available. Vincente, thank you for telling the story. I know it was painful for you.

[The men stand and Sol shakes hands formally with the two of them. He starts to move toward the front door.]

VINCENTE: Mr. Milton, one more thing—

SOL: Yes, Vincente. What is it?

VINCENTE: The last thing that Mr. Rick said, before we helped him up from the floor—

SOL: Yes?

VINCENTE: He said, "Closure…I think we have closure." What do you suppose he meant by that?

[Mario's piano is heard, the volume rising, and he sings:

> *Just in case you miss me too*
> *I'll be there to welcome you*
> *That's why I keep goin' back to Joe's*

Sol looks around with a wry smile, turns slowly and heads for the door as the lights dim.]

The End

A FLOWER IN HER HAIR

from *Monday Update*

The scene stopped Kent in his tracks: a young couple sitting on the hard chairs in the lobby of the business office with Theo, the office manager, towering over them, delivering a lecture. Theo wearing the business uniform of the day—white shirt, striped tie, dark gabardine slacks, polished wingtips—and the couple looking like refugees from the Summer of Love.

It was the young man who initially caught Kent's attention, wearing a hat straight out of Dr. Seuss, a tall black stovepipe that tilted to one side. The girl wore a long cotton dress in a floral pattern and she was barefoot. She wore a flower—a camellia—in her long brown hair. Kent wished he had a camera. The caption to the picture: "Generation Gap."

He watched Theo's animated speech, though he couldn't hear what was said. Now Kent could not take his eyes away from the girl. She was about Maddie's age—eighteen or nineteen—and he wondered what his daughter was doing at that moment. Probably sitting in class at the university, or maybe rushing out of her apartment, heading to her part-time job waiting tables. It had been—what was it?—six months since he'd heard from her. He shook his head and walked away.

Kent's office was on the second floor in the northeast corner of the building. There were windows facing north and east, but there wasn't much to see, unless you had a passion for trains. To the north, just across the street from the building, a cyclone fence separated downtown Roseville, California, from the Southern Pacific rail yard. At one time, this had been the busiest switching center on the West Coast, a convergence of lines coming from the north and east, then heading south through the Central Valley and west toward the Bay Area. Farther west along the tracks were the remains of what was once the largest ice-making facility in the world. Refrigerator cars would be packed with ice to ship fruits and vegetables throughout the western states. Several sets of track ran east and west through the yard. On the far side, two football fields away, was the Old Town section of the city.

Times change, technology changes, but it was still an active switching yard. Kent had learned to live with the constant noise of the engines as they pushed, pulled, and banged freight cars together, assembling trains that would head out to the world. He'd been at his desk about an hour when he decided to call Theo.

"Yeah, Kent, what's up?"

"Not much, Theo. Just wondering what was going on with those kids in the office this morning. You know, the Cat in the Hat."

Theo laughed. "Yeah well, he was lookin' for work. Something temporary. They need money to get to Santa Cruz where the kid has a job lined up. They're newlyweds. Can you believe it? They look like they're sixteen years old, for chrissake."

"So, it looked like you were giving them a stern talking-to. What did you tell them?"

"Nah, I just said we didn't have any temp work, told him to check with some of the other businesses in town."

They chatted a while longer and Kent went back to the stack of papers on his desk. It occurred to him that it was unusually quiet out in the rail yard, nice for a change.

Kent sat at the far end of the counter at Benny's Café, around the corner from the office, enjoying a sandwich and the local newspaper. He glanced at his coffee cup; it was empty. He looked around for Dorothea, the tiny shop's only waitress. She stood near the cash register at the front of the café, locked in conversation with the young man he'd seen that morning, still wearing the odd hat. Outside on the sidewalk, the girl held a leash attached to a large and handsome shepherd mix. The dog drank from a paper cup. Benny came out from the kitchen to join the conversation at the register. Dorothea broke away and approached Kent with a pot of fresh coffee.

"What's all that about?" Kent nodded toward the front of the shop.

"He's looking for work. Kind of a sad story. Says their car was broken into last night while they were staying at the Barker Hotel. Everything they own was taken, including all their wedding gifts. He needs to make some money, for food and gas to get to Santa Cruz...or somewhere."

"Tell you what, let them order whatever they want. I'll pay you later this afternoon, or tomorrow morning. Okay? But don't tell them it's me."

"Okay. I'm sure they're hungry. Thanks, Kent."

"Is Benny gonna let him wash dishes or something?"

"I don't know. Could be."

Kent finished his lunch and paid his bill at the register. The young couple occupied a booth, scanning the menu. If the girl was still barefoot, Benny had decided to look the other way. Outside, the dog sat majestically, his leash tied to a parking meter, eyes fixed on his masters.

Kent wondered if Maddie had ever been in this situation— stranded, hungry, out of money—and if some stranger had paid for her meal? Why was she out of touch, out of sight, off the grid for such long periods of time? Yeah, the phone worked in both directions and he hadn't made the effort to call. The more time that went by, the harder it became to call. *Stupid, stupid, stupid! It's your daughter, for God's sake!* What was wrong? What was the issue? They really needed to talk—soon. He checked his watch and started back toward the office.

———∿∽◦◦◦◦∽∿———

Kent was wrapping up his work day, trying to bring some order to the chaos on his desk. He turned to the credenza to place some files in a drawer. As he did, he looked out the window. On the street below, the young couple and the dog crossed the intersection, headed for a gate in the cyclone fence. Though the gate was locked, the wire fabric had been pulled back creating an opening large enough to crawl through. The hole in the gate had been there as long as Kent could remember; no one bothered to fix it.

The boy went through first, followed by the girl, and then the dog. They stood for a moment and then the boy scooped the girl—still shoeless—up into his arms. With the dog by his side, he started across the tracks, heading for the Barker Hotel over in Old Town. The girl snuggled her head against the boy's neck.

Where would Maddie be right now? Probably getting ready for work. She'd done well as a waitress, working in upscale restaurants, earning good tips. She'd done it all on her own, supporting herself, paying for her education. He was proud of her, very proud. He needed to tell her that.

What was their problem? What issues separated them? These were dumb questions, because Kent knew the answers. After the divorce and his remarriage, he'd thrown himself completely into his new life and new family. At a time when Maddie needed him the most, he wasn't there. There was nothing he could do to change that now. But he needed to say *I'm sorry*, and maybe she needed to hear him say it.

One of Kent's coworkers stuck his head in the door with a

question. The conversation lasted for several minutes. When Kent returned to the window, the odd trio was nowhere in sight.

He stared out at the rail yard, a hundred questions running through his mind. What did they order at Benny's? Did they save any for the dog? Did Benny let the kid wash dishes, or mop floors? Did he earn enough money for gas? Where were they from, and why did they leave, and what about their families? Kent looked for them the next day and the day after that, but he never saw them again.

He couldn't put the girl out of his mind, just a kid with a flower in her hair, a girl about Maddie's age. He picked up the phone, but set it back in the cradle, waiting for the lump in his throat to clear. He picked it up again and punched in Maddie's number. He took a quick breath as it began to ring.

Other Places –
Other Lives

"I have purposely avoided certain places
and have not kept in touch with any of our old buds…
Nevertheless, I have good memories, and good feelings
from that time in our lives
when we were leaving our childhood behind
to begin our lives in the adult world
having only each other to help us find
what would become our way in the world.
In the end, they say, you have nothing but your story.
What a story it has been!"

-Ron DeSellier,
December, 2014

EUREKA

from *Monday Update*

A full moon hung over the Trinity River Valley in Northern California. It made for a beautiful drive—the moonlight on the water, the gentle slope of the canyon lined with pines, the river like a rippling white ribbon. Ward glanced up from the winding road, determined to print the scene in his mind. He'd never seen a picture so perfect. He figured he'd be in Eureka around 10:00 p.m., get a room there and take a long, hot soak in the tub and then a shower. After camping for five days on the Trinity, a hot bath and a warm bed seemed like heaven.

He had left Jimmy in Junction City at Pat's place. Jimmy would be heading home tomorrow, back to Redding and down through the long valley to Vallejo. They had fished the Trinity hard, from Weaverville to Junction City, with nothing to show for it this year. Nineteen seventy-three was not a banner year for salmon. That didn't matter. October on the Trinity was reward enough: the clear, cold mornings out on the water, the afternoon temperatures climbing into the eighties, the air so fresh you could taste it, and then hanging out at the bar Pat owned where cold beer and conversation flowed like the river itself. The fishing didn't matter.

This was his last trip with Jimmy, Karyn's father. That's what mattered. Karyn was moving on and there was no way to change that. She was in love, and you can't fight love. You can't say *don't love him, love me*. It doesn't work that way. It was good of Jimmy to plan the trip, their last hoorah so to speak. They had fished the Trinity for salmon every fall for a half-dozen years and this trip was a nice nod to tradition. Jimmy was a good man, damn good, and he'd been a great father-in-law. For the five days they were together, he'd never mentioned Karyn, never asked about the break-up. Ward was grateful. He didn't want to talk about it.

———∿∿⚬⚬⌒⚬⚬⌒⚬⚬∿∿———

Ward made it to Eureka on schedule and found a room at a motel on West Fifth Street. After the hot soak and shower, he felt like a new man. He was ready to find a friendly tavern and throw back a cold beer or two. The attendant at the front desk directed him to a place a couple of blocks over, an easy walk from the motel.

The night air was cool, fog beginning to roll in across Humboldt Bay, when Ward reached the bar situated on a corner. He was about to cross the street when a car came tearing down the hill from his right and lurched to a stop at the curb. A girl with short blonde hair leaned out of the passenger side window, laughing and shouting. The driver, a woman who looked to be a little older, jumped out of the car and helped the blonde out of the front seat. Together they stormed through the door of the bar.

Ward wasn't looking for excitement. He thought about turning around and heading back to his room. Finally he crossed the street and went inside. There were a handful of customers at the bar and in booths along the wall. A small dance floor took up the back of the room, a jukebox off to one side. He took a stool and waited.

The bartender was busy with the two recent arrivals, especially the blonde girl. She was talking loud, laughing, poking fun at him, and he was giving it right back to her. It seemed they knew each other. She stood on her stool and leaned across the bar, showing generous cleavage from a scoop-neck knit top, and demanded a kiss from the barkeep. He grabbed a breast in each hand and planted a kiss on her lips, all the while squeezing the ripe little peaches. The blonde girl found this hilarious. What strange world had Ward stumbled into?

The bartender broke away and came toward him. "Hey, buddy! What can I get you?"

"Whatever you have on tap. Hey, what's with the wild child over there?"

"Oh, don't worry about her." He smiled. "Her sister is keepin' an eye on her."

So that was it: little sister, big sister. Ward nursed his beer and tried to relax. He noticed the girl glancing his way every now and then. After a couple of rounds, she was starting to look pretty good. She was a little plump, spilling over her jeans at the waist, but she had a pleasant face and large, expressive eyes. It really was a nice face. You'd have to say pretty if you were being fair. She smiled at him once when their eyes met and she had a nice smile, too. Another couple of beers and she would look like a young Shirley Jones. The *Partridge Family* theme played in his head.

Ward took some change and wandered over to the jukebox. It was a good playlist and he dropped in a few quarters and started to punch in his picks. And then the girl was standing next to him, bumping elbows.

"Why don'tcha play 'Earth Angel'? I love that song."

"Sure." He punched in the letter-number combination, wondering at the choice, a song from the mid-fifties. "Anything else?"

They scanned the columns and made a few more selections. She was very young. Was she old enough to be in this place? He got a strong whiff of cologne, mixed with the alcohol on her breath, and he recognized the scent: it was Karyn's favorite. What was it called? Emerald, or Emeraude, something like that. This girl had bathed in it.

"I'm Ward, by the way." He waited for her to respond. "And you are?"

"Umm, I'm Jane. Call me Jane."

"Jane Doe?"

"What?"

"Nothing. Can I buy you and your friend a drink?"

"Sure." She led the way over to the bar. "This here's my sister. What'd you say your name was?"

"Ward."

"This here's Ward. He's gonna buy us a drink."

Big sister gave Ward a critical glance and then nodded. She had no name she wanted to share. She was drinking club soda. Jane ordered a 7-and-7. They sat through several rounds and chatted about nothing in particular. Big Sister kept her eyes straight ahead, chain smoking and sipping her soda. She had nothing to say. "Earth Angel" came on the jukebox again.

"Oh, come on, let's dance." Jane grabbed Ward's arm. "I love this song."

They slow-danced to "Earth Angel," and then to two more ballads. By the third song, Jane was wrapped around him and Ward couldn't help but be aroused. He knew she could feel it but she didn't pull away. He was lightheaded from all the beer. Or was it the cologne? As the music ended, she reached up to him, her lips parted, and he kissed her long and deep. When she stepped back, there were tears in her eyes.

"Hey, what's wrong?"

"Nothin'."

"Come on, I thought we were having a good time."

"It's not you, Ned—"

"Ward."

"Ward…sorry. I'm thinking about my old man, my boyfriend. He's doin' six months in county. I really miss him."

"Sorry to hear that." He started to ask *six months for what?* but he didn't want to know. "Come on, let's have another drink. Maybe you'll feel better." He led her back to the bar and ordered another round.

"I really feel bad, ya know? I miss him. He's not a bad guy. He was always good to me."

"Well, maybe he'll get out early, good behavior or something." Ward glanced at Big Sister who gave him a look that said *Yeah, sure.*

"But I feel bad, 'cause while he's been in there, I chippied on him. I chippied on him a lot."

Ward thought he knew what "chippied" meant, but he wasn't sure and he didn't want to ask. It was time to take a trip to the men's room and splash a little water in his face. He excused himself and made his way down the narrow hall past the dance floor.

As he washed his hands, he noticed the condom vending machine mounted on the wall. He thought about the kiss on the dance floor and imagined taking that warm young body to his bed. He dried his hands, dropped in the required coins and stuffed the foil packets into the pocket of his jeans.

When he returned to the bar, Jane was gone. Big Sis was there, chain smoking and fixing him with a steady gaze. She turned on her stool to face him.

"Watch yourself, *Ward*." Her voice was calm and cool, but she pronounced his name like an exclamation point. She was about Ward's age—mid-thirties—and though her hair was dark, the resemblance to her sister was clear.

"What?"

"You heard me. Watch yourself. She's just a kid, a kid with problems. The last thing she needs is a one night stand with a jerk like you."

"Look, I don't know what you think—"

"You think it's going to be easy, a sure thing. Right, *Ward*? You'll just say, 'Hubba hubba, baby. Let's go back to my place. I'll show you a real good time.'"

"No, I mean, come on..." He glanced around as though looking for help. He could not look her in the eye.

"And what's your story, *Ward*? Divorced? Separated? Yeah, I noticed the little tan line on your ring finger."

He covered his left hand with his right.

"And now you think you're God's gift to wayward girls?" She punctuated the question with a wry smile.

"Look, Big Sister...sorry, I didn't catch your name."

"My name doesn't matter, *Ward*. Let's just say I'm your conscience, here to make sure you do the right thing."

"Which is?"

"Leave now, while she's still in the ladies room. Go back to wherever you're staying, watch some porn, whack off, do whatever it is that you do. And *leave my sister alone*." She let it sink in for a few seconds. "Don't worry, I'll tell her you said goodbye, good luck, best wishes. All that crap."

There was nothing more to say. He'd been busted and he was no match for this woman. He got up off the stool, dropped a few dollars on the bar, and headed for the door, away from this strange encounter in Eureka.

———

Ward checked out early the next morning. He popped the tailgate and tossed his bag into the back of the compact wagon. As he stuffed his dirty clothes in among the camping gear, he saw the shirt he'd been wearing the night before. He picked it up and brought it to his nose. It smelled of cigarettes and cologne. He paused to play back the events at the bar and felt the blood rush to his cheeks. Big Sister, God bless her, had been right.

Ward sniffed the shirt again, then closed his eyes, and just for a moment Karyn was there. She had not been with him all week on the Trinity, but now she was. He started to say her name, but his throat tightened. He'd lost her, and now he was out here on his own, acting the fool.

He wadded the shirt into a tight ball and threw it—hard—into the back of the car. His shout became a howl, echoing through the parking lot and down Fifth Street until the air was gone from his lungs.

It was time to move on, time to forget, and that scent carried memories.

Ten Thousand Lakes

from *Monday Update*

I t was one of those jaw-dropping, Oh-my-God, small-world happenings, the kind you remember and talk about years later. I'd gone to the counter with my check and handed the pretty hostess my credit card. She ran it through the machine that stamped the information on a multi-copy receipt form. This was 1962, well before there was a handy network to swipe your card for instant approval. She wrote the amount on the form and handed it to me. I filled in the tip and the total and signed the receipt.

She smiled and gave me my card. "Gary Bracken? I knew a Gary Bracken when I was a little girl."

I smiled back. "Oh really? I'm from California."

"Vallejo, California?" she said. We stopped dead still and stared at each other. "Gary Bracken…who lived on Laurel Street?"

"Yeah," I said.

"Gary, I'm Nancy Gilkey. Do you remember me?"

As I said: jaw-dropping, Oh-my-God, what a small world.

She came out from behind the counter and hugged me and the words tumbled out of our mouths. All the while a small line was forming behind me, people waiting to pay their checks. She wrote her telephone number on a scrap of paper and we agreed that I'd call her and we'd get together for coffee or something.

I'd gone into Hasty Tasty, a bright, clean, well-run restaurant on Lake Street just west of Hennepin in Minneapolis, for my favorite—fresh-baked apple pie with French vanilla ice cream—and I'd come away with Nancy Gilkey's phone number. It had been about twenty years since we'd last seen each other. We were both six years old when her family moved away. She was a Navy brat, her father some sort of ranking administrator stationed at the Naval Hospital on Mare Island. His orders came through and they were gone. But Nancy Gilkey would never be forgotten.

My apartment was just a short walk from the corner of Hennepin and Lake. On the way home, the scenes from our childhood played back in my mind and blood rushed to my cheeks. Nancy's family didn't stay long in Vallejo, just long enough for her to attend kindergarten and first grade. The Gilkeys lived across the street and for that brief period of time I was her favorite playmate. Their home was a split-level with a flight of stairs that led up to the front door. Under that stairwell was an open space, accessible from inside the garage. Most people used this space for storage, but Nancy had turned it into a playroom. A toy stove, cups and dishes, plastic knives, forks and spoons, dolls with assorted clothing—the perfect space for playing house. There wasn't much light, just the daylight that came through the screened air vent, and there was barely enough room to stand up. Still it was a great place to while away the hours playing whatever game Nancy invented. She was a born leader at age six and I was the perfect follower.

That was the problem.

We were playing barbershop one day, a pillow case pinned around my neck while Nancy did an excellent job of trimming the straight brown hair that hung down over my eyebrows. Then it was my turn. Nancy's mom generally braided her long blonde hair into two thick braids, one on either side, then wound and pinned them into a bun at the back of her head. I managed to slip the scissors under the braid on the right side and cut it off. I knew right away this was trouble. I got out of there and ran for home.

But this was not something we could hide. Half of her beautiful blonde hair was gone.

I remember her dad and mine having a long intense conversation out in front of our house. When my dad came in, he put me over his knee and warmed my backside in a way I wouldn't soon forget. My parents decided that I needed to play with my boy friends in the neighborhood and not spend so much time with Nancy. It wasn't long after that when her family moved away.

She took with her the secret of another play day under the stairs, one I'm confident she never told her parents. I certainly never told mine. It happened a week or so before the hair-cutting incident. The game that day was Doctor. Nancy had a little black bag with a play stethoscope, a thermometer, a tongue depressor, and little bottles representing different kinds of medicine. I was the doctor, listening to her heart and so forth. Then she insisted that I had to examine her private parts. Before I could object, she slid down her shorts and her underwear. I'm sure my eyes were like saucers. Then she told me I had to do the same. I knew this wasn't what doctors did, but I followed instructions and dropped my drawers too. We examined each other for a few seconds. There was no touching, but Nancy kept up a steady stream of commentary. I remember she said that hers was pretty and mine wasn't.

Funny how you never forget a comment like that.

———∿∿≈≈≈∿∿———

A week went by and I still hadn't called Nancy. The total recall of our history was embarrassing, even twenty years later. But I was sure we'd run into each other in the neighborhood, so I swallowed hard and called her. We made a date to get together for lunch at The Duet, a coffee shop on Hennepin, just north of Lake.

The Duet was very small, with a row of booths on either side as you entered, and a few tables with hard-backed chairs in the middle of the room. What I remember most about the place was that it was spotless. Nancy was bright and chatty and I felt at ease right away.

"So, Nancy, why Minnesota? What brought you to the Twin Cities?"

"I enrolled at the University of Minnesota. I was there for a couple of semesters but then I dropped out. I really didn't know what I wanted to do, what I wanted to major in. Then I met Joe Smith and fell in love." She smiled and laughed a little.

Joe Smith (not his real name) was a wide receiver for the Minnesota Vikings. I was pretty sure I'd read he was married, but I didn't mention it.

"We eventually moved in together," she continued, "just down the block at Calhoun Terrace. It's a great place, a nice view of the lake, there's a pool on the roof, believe it or not. You'll have to come by some day, take a swim."

The Vikings were about to begin their second season in the Twin Cities and they were the hottest ticket in town. They were entering the season with great expectations driven by exciting young players like Fran Tarkenton and Tommy Mason, veterans like Hugh McElhenny, and a defensive back named Robert Reed who hailed from Vallejo. Their coach was none other than Norm Van Brocklin, "The Dutchman," a Hall of Fame quarterback. Hopes were running high.

"How about you, Gary? What brought you to Minnesota? Not the usual choice for a California kid."

"Yeah, well, I came following a girl. She was also a student at U-of-M. I got a job with Northwest Airlines out at the airport and we lived together for a while."

"And then?"

"She changed her mind. About me and the University. The last I heard, she was back East somewhere. At Georgetown, I think."

"But you stayed?"

"Yeah, I have to admit, I fell in love with Minneapolis, especially this neighborhood."

On that point, Nancy and I were in complete agreement. Within the radius of a few blocks you had everything you needed for living in the city. There were good restaurants, a fine supermarket, the Uptown Theater (if you didn't mind second-run movies), and you were close to Lake Calhoun and Lake of the Isles, part of a lovely chain of lakes that ran through the south side of town.

Our lunch lasted almost three hours, and the conversation never lagged.

—————⟶⟶⟶⟶—————

Nancy and I got together regularly after that, not only for meals but lots of other activities. When Joe was on the road for a game, she had plenty of free time. We'd rent bicycles and ride around the lakes, or rent a canoe and paddle our way around. We'd go to movies at the Uptown, or just walk through the neighborhood, one of my favorite things to do. We'd stop at the Uptown where there was a tiny shop out on the sidewalk that sold popcorn and candy. The old man who ran the shop also kept bags of roasted-in-the-shell peanuts in the popcorn machine case where they stayed nice and warm. There was nothing like those warm, salty peanuts as you walked along the tree-lined streets.

I began to see Nancy in a different light. She was sensitive, kind, intelligent, funny, and infinitely curious about the world around her. She was also beautiful, no question about that, even with her hair stuffed under a baseball cap or blowing wild in the wind, wearing faded jeans, beat-up Keds, and not a drop of makeup. And then there was me with my movie star looks; that is if Buddy Hackett was your ideal movie star.

We were an odd pair.

Those fall days are a warm memory, one I return to again and again. My feelings for Nancy were changing. I wanted to be more than just the guy who filled the hours when Joe was out of town.

As we spent time together, Nancy opened up a little and told me that Joe's wife and kids lived in Los Angeles. The kids were in great schools and they chose not to disrupt them by moving to Minnesota. The hard winters were another factor. And that's all she said; nothing about hopes or plans for herself and Joe.

———— ~wooerooroowv ————

The Vikings had a road game in Los Angeles on Sunday, October 21. That Saturday night, my phone rang; it was Nancy.

"Hi, Gary. I hate to ask, but can I crash with you for a few days?"

I said, "Sure, what's up?"

"Joe's wife is flying back from L.A. with the team. She's going to spend a week in the Twin Cities. Joe told me to make myself scarce. Do you mind? I don't want to go to a hotel and I've got nowhere else to go."

"Not a problem. You can have the couch."

She showed up later with two large suitcases in tow. My heart broke for her. She was very quiet and withdrawn the rest of that night and all day Sunday. We made it a point not to watch the game on TV.

The Vikings won, by the way.

We both had Monday off and so we went downtown to the Walker Museum and took in a terrific exhibit of Brazilian art. The artists' names are lost to memory but I can still picture the large canvases splashed with vivid colors, an explosion of reds, greens, and blues that made me think of an abstract riot in a jungle.

That evening, we sat mesmerized in front of the television while President Kennedy made an address to the nation about the Soviet Union installing ballistic missiles in Cuba. He announced a "quarantine" of all ships bound for Cuba bearing offensive weapons and the truth of the situation began to sink in.

We were balanced on the razor's edge of a nuclear war.

The next day, when I drove to work at the airport, a row of Strategic Air Command bombers lined the tarmac at the Air National Guard facility across from the passenger terminal. I stopped the car and stared for a few minutes. What event would cause those flying giants to scramble? What routes would they fly and what cities in the U.S.S.R. would they target? And what about Soviet planes and missiles pointed our way? Were the Twin Cities on their target list?

When I got home Tuesday evening, Nancy was sitting at the little table in the kitchen, a glass of red wine in front of her, a half-empty bottle on the table. She invited me to join her, so I took a glass out of the cupboard and pulled up a chair. We talked quietly, killed the bottle, and then opened another.

"I'm not going back to Joe," she said. "It's over between us." I knew from the tone of her voice that she meant it.

"Good decision, Nance. So what will you do?" I didn't add *Assuming we're all still alive in the days and weeks ahead.*

"My parents are living in Norfolk now. I could go home, but I hate to think about it. Stupid pride, I guess. They told me from the beginning that I was making a mistake."

And there we sat, two people feeling very little control over what might happen next in our lives, both of us getting sloshed on that nice red wine. Then she started to laugh.

"Remember when you cut off my braid?"

I nearly choked on my wine and started laughing too.

"And remember when we played doctor?"

"Of course I remember. You said yours was pretty and mine wasn't. That scarred me for life!"

We were both laughing hard now and it went on for a minute or so, until I realized she had buried her face in her hands and was sobbing. I went around the table, knelt by her chair and gathered her in my arms. I held her until the sobbing subsided and she was able to speak.

"How could I be such an idiot? He doesn't care about me.

I'm just his roadie, his girl away from home. How could I be so stupid?"

"Look," I said, "you'll stay here as long as you want, until you figure out what to do. You can even have the bedroom and I'll take the couch."

I guess it was the right thing to say because that's when the kissing started. Later she led me to the bedroom and made love to me in a way I would never forget. Nancy Gilkey had a gift for unforgettable moments.

The next morning, after several cups of coffee, we sat down to talk. Nancy said our night together was a mistake, a combination of too much wine, a bad breakup, and a feeling of *We're all doomed so what the hell.* She was leading again, just as she had when we were six years old, and I chose to follow. I didn't declare my feelings, afraid I'd screw things up, maybe ruin our friendship. Instead, I agreed with Nancy's assessment.

I invited her to stay on as my roommate. She said yes.

———⟶∿∽∞⟋⟋⟋∽∿———

You're probably wondering how it all turned out. Well, the Vikings had a miserable season: two wins, eleven losses, one tie. Joe got less and less playing time and was finally traded to another team.

Nikita Khrushchev openly backed down and removed his missiles from Cuba in exchange for a promise the U.S. would not invade the island. Kennedy also quietly removed our missiles from Italy and Turkey. Most people saw JFK as a hero for his handling of the crisis. Of course we couldn't know he had little more than a year to live.

Nancy stayed for about a month, then swallowed her pride and went home to Norfolk. Later she enrolled at the University of Virginia in Charlottesville where she earned an advanced degree, met her soul mate, got married and settled down to raise a family.

For many years, I would receive a card at Christmastime, generally with a short note and a family photo. I enjoyed comparing the annual pictures of her children, watching them grow into handsome young adults.

As for me, life has been good. Let's leave it at that. But when anyone sets out to tell me a *small world* story, I listen politely, but all the while I'm thinking *Nancy Gilkey...Nancy Gilkey.*

REUNION

The bar at the Elks Club was thirty feet long with shorter sections at each end, shaped like a long, flat U. I stepped up to one end and tried to get a bartender's attention, in between stopping to shake hands and say hello to old classmates. It was the forty-fifth reunion of the Class of '60.

Down at the other end of the bar, someone caught my eye. Sure enough, it was Zach. He was straight and tall as ever, about six four, and he'd aged well from what I could see. Zach was one of those guys that seemed to get better looking with age. He had a real Clint Eastwood thing going on.

I thought about the hours and hours of basketball we'd played together, all through middle school and high school. Zach was our center, and a pretty good one, while I played guard. We weren't bad for a couple of white guys who couldn't jump, and we'd logged a lot of good memories. That was on the basketball court.

Off the court? Well, that was another story.

Zach and I fell for the same girl, a gorgeous little brunette named Marissa. Zach and Marissa had been together for a couple of years when she broke up with him. That was when we were seniors. I asked her out, way too soon in Zach's mind, and she and I dated for a couple of months, just long enough for me to fall head over heels. But Marissa had other plans, and though she tried to let me down gently, I landed pretty hard.

In a perfect world, the three of us would have gone our

separate ways, no hard feelings, have a good life. That's not the way it worked out. Zach never spoke to me again.

Zach stayed in our hometown and founded a couple of successful businesses. I moved away and tried to build a career in information technology. He married another girl from our class and lived happily ever after. I wasn't so lucky, but that's a story for another time.

So there I stood, staring at Zach, way down at the other end of the bar. I forgot about flagging down a bartender. And then Zach looked up and our eyes met. A little smile crossed his face, and all I could remember in that moment were the good times we'd shared, competing together, winning and losing, but always together.

I did a strange thing, something I'd never done before. I raised my right hand above my head, my arm outstretched, my fist clenched, like something out of *Dances with Wolves*, some sort of blood-brother salute. Zach smiled again, and then he spread his arms straight out to the left and right, a giant invitation to a hug. I stood up from my stool, so did he, and we met halfway down the long bar. He wrapped me in a great bear hug and lifted me off the floor.

Zach and I got rip-roaring drunk that night and the Elks sent me back to my hotel in a cab. We've stayed in touch ever since, and every time I see him, he crushes me in that great hug.

We never talk about Marissa.

Pipe Dream

from *Monday Update*

"What?! You met Babe Ruth?"

"Yep. Met him twice."

My grandfather sat back in his favorite chair, his legs up on the ottoman, puffed on his pipe and gave me a wry smile. I had just mentioned that I'd met Bill Gates once, at a bridge tournament in Sacramento. I'd played my Bill Gates card and Gramps topped me with two Babe Ruths.

"Grandpa, why haven't I heard this story before?"

"Well, Lonnie ... I guess you never asked."

He smiled again, obviously enjoying the moment. My grandfather, Alton Blaire Jacobs, was a storyteller. He loved nothing more than to hold you spellbound while he spun a good tale, and he loved to take his time, every sentence punctuated by a few puffs on his favorite pipe. In fact, when you see "..." below, you can read "puff puff puff."

Now I was hooked. I had to hear this story. But Gramps was having fun, toying with me, waiting for me to ask.

"Okay, Gramps, you've gotta tell me. I'm all ears. How did you meet Babe Ruth?"

"Well ... the first time was in Chicago, October 1, 1932. I remember that date because it was the evening after the third game of the 1932 World Series. I was just a kid, working as a busboy at a restaurant called The Ivanhoe … It was just a few blocks south of Wrigley Field at Clark and Wellington."

"Yeah? So what happened?" It was clear that breaks to puff on his pipe were going to be a major feature of this yarn.

"Well … I was near the front desk, it was still early, the dinner crowd wouldn't start showing up till seven or eight, and this man came through the front door with a big grin on his face. He was about five nine with a powerful build, wearing a dark suit and a gray fedora, and he clapped a hand on my shoulder and said, 'Son, is Frank Pieper here?' You see, Frank 'Pat' Pieper was the maître d' at The Ivanhoe … He was also the field announcer for the Chicago Cubs and the Cubbies were playing the Yankees in the '32 Series. I said, 'You mean Pat Pieper? Yeah, he's in the back. Can I give him your name?' He grinned and said, 'Yeah, tell him Francesco Pezzolo is here to see him.'"

Gramps paused again.

"And? What then?" I felt like I was pulling teeth.

"Well … I went into the back room where Pat was getting ready, going over the reserved tables and such, and I said, 'Mr. Pieper, there's a Francesco Pezzolo here to see you.' He said, 'Francesco Pezzolo? Well I'll be damned, it's Ping! Ping Bodie!' Pat hurried out to the front, me right behind him, and he and Ping hugged each other like long lost brothers. They were laughin' and cuttin' up and I couldn't help but smile to watch them … It turns out that Ping started his major league career across town with the White Sox back in 1911. He was with the Sox through 1914, and the two of them, Pat and Ping, got to know each other. Pat started with the Cubs as a vendor at the West Side Grounds in 1904."

"But wait, who was Francesco…whatshisname?"

"Ha! You see, Ping was born Francesco Pezzolo and grew up in San Francisco. Now, Bodie, California, was a rowdy mining town in the eastern Sierras with nearly as many bars and brothels as citizens, a real tough place. Apparently this made a big impression, because Francesco Pezzolo changed his name to Frank Bodie.

'Ping' was his nickname for the sound of his fifty-two ounce bat when he connected with a baseball."

"Okay. So where does The Babe come into this?"

"Be patient, Lonnie. I'm gettin' there."

My grandfather's pipe had gone out, and he took a minute to refill and light it. He always bought a special blend of tobacco from a local shop and it had a sweet, pleasant aroma that filled the room.

"Where was I? Oh … so, it turns out after Ping left the White Sox, he eventually signed with the Yankees. Played with the Yanks from 1918 to 1921. He was Babe Ruth's first roommate. His first roommate, Lonnie! And Ping's the one who gave him the nickname 'Bambino.'"

"That's amazing."

"So … Ping was in town for the World Series as Babe's guest, and he was at The Ivanhoe looking for a place where Ruth and some of the guys could take their wives for drinks and dinner. Ping wanted to know if Pat could handle a group of eight or ten later that evening. Remember now, this was right at the end of Prohibition and alcohol was still illegal. But … The Ivanhoe had a cellar speakeasy known as The Catacombs, one of the best stocked joints on the North Side."

"Geez, Gramps! You worked in a Chicago speakeasy during Prohibition?"

"Yep. Served everybody from the mayor to the police commissioner at one time or another … So, Pat said, 'Hell yes, tell The Babe to come on down. I'll take good care of 'em, even if they are the Yankees.' They had a good laugh over that one, talked for a while longer, and then Ping said goodbye … Well, Pat sent me off to make sure we had plenty of the best Canadian whiskey and good local beer, and to set up a private room down in The Catacombs where Babe's group wouldn't be bothered."

Gramps took a few puffs and looked off into space. I was on the edge of my chair. "So? What happened then?"

"Well ... It got to be nine, nine thirty, and Pat was gettin' worried. We were primed and ready. The kitchen was alerted. Pat had his best waiters standing by. He'd even called the *Sun Times* to let their man-about-town columnist know that the Yankees would be coming to The Ivanhoe. Finally, a little before ten, there was a big commotion in the foyer. The Babe and his group came on like Gang Busters. I've never seen an entrance like that, before or since. I tell you, Lonnie, it was something."

"Is that when you met him?"

"No ... that came later, when Babe was looking for the men's room and I showed him the way. I told him I was a big fan, even though I was for the Cubs in the Series. He was in a great mood, with the Yanks up three games to none, and he just laughed and shook my hand, asked me what I was up to besides working at The Ivanhoe. I told him I was a student at Northwestern, working my way through college. Boy, was that the right thing to say. After that, every time I came near their table, to refill water glasses or pick up plates or something, they were stuffing my pockets with dollar bills. It turned out to be the best payday of my young life."

"So who was there, in Babe's party?"

"There was Babe and his wife Claire. And Ping Bodie, of course. Lefty Gomez, Tony Lazzeri, Frankie Corsetti, and their wives. Bodie, Lazzeri, and Crosetti were all from San Francisco, and Gomez was also from the Bay Area. Those guys all came up through the Frisco Seals in the Pacific Coast League."

"That's some group."

"And ya know, for all the stories about Babe Ruth and his shenanigans, they were a well-behaved bunch. Oh, they were tellin' stories and laughin' loud, but nobody was out of line, Lonnie. Not a one."

"But didn't they have a game the next day?"

"Oh, yeah. But that didn't bother 'em. And you know, the Yanks won the fourth game to sweep the Series. But I'm just getting to the best part, Lonnie ... There were some guys from the press that dropped by during the evening to have a drink and hang out with The Babe. One of 'em was Joe Williams who was with the *New York World Telegram*. He came over to talk with Pat, and I was there stacking plates. He said, 'Hey, Pat, what about Ruth's home run in the fifth?' Pat said, 'Hardest hit ball I've ever seen at Wrigley, Joe.' Williams says, 'Yeah, but did you see him point to the stands before the pitch?' 'Hell yeah, I saw it! I had the best seat in the house. I not only saw him point, I heard him barkin' at Guy Bush in the Cubs dugout. *That's two strikes, but watch this, you s.o.b.* Charlie Root came in with a fat one and wham, it was gone.' Williams said, 'Wait till you see my write-up tomorrow morning, Pat. Ha! I tell ya, this story has legs.'"

"So what did Williams write, Gramps?"

"The headline was 'RUTH CALLS SHOT AS HE PUTS HOME RUN NO. 2 IN SIDE POCKET.' And that's how it was christened the Called Shot Home Run. I picked up the *World Telegram* at a newsstand near the ballpark the next day, and if I had any sense, I would have saved it, Lonnie. There's always been controversy. Some folks say Babe called his shot, others say he didn't. But I've always believed Pat Pieper's account. You know his station with the brand new public address system at Wrigley was on the field, next to the backstop on the third base side. He really did have the best seat in the house."

"So that was the first time. When was the second time you met The Babe?"

"You know, Lonnie, all this talk is makin' me thirsty. There's some Canadian Club in the cabinet over there. Will you join me?"

"Sure, Gramps. How do you take it?"

"Two fingers, three rocks. Glasses are in the kitchen, ice is in the freezer."

He smiled as I hurried away to fix the drinks. It wasn't surprising that I hadn't heard this story. My grandfather finished his career with McDonnell-Douglas in St. Louis in the late seventies. He decided that Chicago was home and that's where he retired. I'd grown up in Southern California, and though we saw him and Grams two or three times a year, I'm sure there were a hundred tales I hadn't heard.

I brought the drinks into the living room and settled in to hear the rest of the story. He raised his glass to me and did his Bogart impression, always good for a laugh.

"Here's looking at you, kid. Now, where was I?"

"You met Ping Bodie and Babe Ruth on October 1, 1932, Joe Williams coined the phrase Called Shot Home Run, and Pat Pieper swears he not only saw it, he heard it."

"Yep, that pretty well sums it up, all right ... So, move ahead to March, 1948. The Babe had been retired for a dozen years or so, and he'd been diagnosed with throat cancer. Hollywood was rushing to make a movie of his life, *The Babe Ruth Story*, starring William Bendix. I was working for Douglas Aircraft in L.A. at the time and I'd kept in touch with Pat Pieper over the years, birthday cards, Christmas Cards and the like. Pat was taking a vacation trip to California before the start of the '48 season and he got in touch, invited me to join him for lunch at the Brown Derby on Wilshire. And guess who else was coming to lunch?"

"Yeah, go on."

"Ping Bodie, who was working as an electrician at Universal Studios, and The Babe himself. He was in L.A. to visit the movie set."

"Geez, unbelievable."

"Yep ... Well, we met at the Brown Derby and Pat and Ping looked great. Healthy, full of P-and-V. But Ruth looked bad. He was a big man, you know, six two, two fifty. But he looked smaller, he'd lost a lot of weight, and his voice was just a rasp. Still, he had that mischief about him, always ready for a laugh. I mostly kept my mouth shut and listened to the three of them tell stories. But I did get in a question. I said, 'Babe, what do you think of William Bendix playing you in the movie?' He laughed and said, 'Hell, they got the homeliest guy in Hollywood to play me. Am I that ugly? Don't answer that!' We were all laughing then."

"Go on, Gramps."

"Well, The Babe left the table for a few minutes and I asked Ping what it was like to be his roommate. Ping said, 'Oh, I never saw much of the Bambino. He always had somewhere to go, somebody a lot prettier than me to be with. Hell, I mostly roomed with his suitcase.' That's a great line, eh Lonnie? I laughed hard at that one."

"And then?"

"That was about it. We were standing on the sidewalk out in front of the Derby and Ping said, 'Where you headed now, Pat?' Pat said, 'Up to Northern Cal. I've got three sisters living up there in a shipyard town called Vallejo.' Ping said, 'The hell you say! My son and his family live there. He works on the shipyard.'"

"Wow. What a small world."

"Small indeed, Lonnie … We said goodbye to Ping and Babe and watched them walk away toward the parking lot. But I had one last question. I said, 'Pat, did Babe really call his shot off Charlie Root back in '32?' 'Oh hell yes, Alton. Just like I've always said. And don't let anyone tell you different.' Then Pat turned to look at me. He winked and said, 'Ya know, if you want to be remembered, it's best to be on the right side of a great story.' Well … I walked Pat back to the Ambassador Hotel, which was just down the block, and said goodbye. That was the last time I saw him, though we stayed in touch. He was with the Cubs until he passed away in 1974."

"That's quite a tale, Gramps. And it's all true?"

"Just like I told you, Lonnie." He smiled and winked. "The right side of a great story."

That visit with my grandfather took place in 1999 when he

was eighty-seven years old. I've checked everything he told me and I can't find any holes. It's all plausible. Just four guys—Ping Bodie, Pat Pieper, Babe Ruth, and Alton Jacobs—and some shared history. So I tell my grandkids, "You know, I met Bill Gates one time, at a bridge tournament in Sacramento. But your great grandfather met Babe Ruth. Twice!"

Believe me, they're impressed—with Bill Gates.

—⁓⧲⁓⁓—

Note: Frank A. Bodie and I met in 1952 when we were drafted onto the same Little League team. We reconnected in 2008 and became close friends. The two of us collaborated on this story, which revolves around the question: did my uncle, Pat Pieper, know Frank's grandfather, Ping Bodie? They were part of the Major League Baseball community in Chicago at a time when that community was very small. With fiction, anything is possible. And so we decided they not only knew each other, they were good friends. My dear friend Frank passed away March 1, 2017. This story is dedicated to his memory.

Fireworks for Mickey

from *Monday Update*

T he cars swerved onto the apron of the road, skidding to a halt in the gravel. Doors flew open and we hit the ground running, sprinting out onto the bridge. We tore open the box of fireworks and went at it—firecrackers popping, cherry bombs and M-80s exploding, bottle rockets and fountains shooting into the air, sending bursts of color into the midnight sky. The river rushed below us, tumbling rapids reflecting the rainbow of the explosions.

It was glorious and wild and beautiful, and the fact that most of us were buzzed added to the sensation. None of the fireworks were legal, but we were not worried. My older brother Randy was the county sheriff and had promised to keep his patrol cars away for a least an hour. We would empty the box before then, stagger back to the cars and peel out, tires screeching, gravel flying, heading down the river road to a place on the bank where we could finish our beer, laughing, shouting, pushing and hugging each other, behaving like tomorrow and its hangover would never come.

Crazy, reckless, dangerous—call it what you want. Mickey would have loved it.

———ᘐᘏᓿᘏᘐ———

It started in my parents' kitchen, a group of us gathered around leaning on the counters, drinking wine and beer and talking about Mickey. The house was full of family and friends gathered after Mickey's funeral, come to share food and drink and stories, so many stories.

Mickey is—was—my younger brother. He died in a water skiing accident at the lake just outside of town. He took a hard fall, hit a submerged log and crushed his chest. It was too soon after a summer storm to be skiing, with so much debris washed out of the creeks and into the lake. But that was Mickey, always living on the edge, pushing the envelope until it burst. He was twenty-eight years old.

It's safe to say everybody loved Mickey. Oh, maybe there were a few who were jealous of the way he stormed through the world, always the life of the party, always the guy with the prettiest girl on his arm, always the star of the winning team, grinning from page one of the sports section with the trophy in his hand.

Mickey! Even his name had a story. My father named him for Mickey Mantle, his all-time favorite ballplayer. It was easy to be jealous of a guy like my brother, but people loved him anyway, because he didn't have an ounce of meanness in him. Even the girls he loved and left never held it against him. Think about that for a minute.

So there we were in the kitchen, talking, laughing, telling Mickey stories, when Patsy Keller came into the room. I recognized her right away, even though her auburn hair was shorter and she no longer wore the horn-rimmed glasses that I thought were so cute and sexy back in high school. I caught her eye and she smiled at me. She crossed the room, took my hand and led me out onto the patio where we could talk. She was one of Mickey's girls; at least I thought she was. They had dated for a while, which broke my heart at the time because I had a huge crush on Patsy Keller. Out on the patio, on this warm July evening, she put her arms around me and held me close. When she stepped back, there were tears in her eyes.

"Bart, I am so sorry about Mickey. How are you doing? How are your parents holding up?"

"I guess we're doing okay. It's really hard on my parents, especially my dad. It's hard to believe Mickey is gone. He was like a force of nature. But I don't have to tell you that. You two were a couple, for a while at least."

She smiled at the suggestion. "No, not really. We had a few dates, but I wasn't Mickey's type. Cheerleaders were more his style. I'm sure I was the only nerd he ever dated."

The only nerd Mickey ever dated? I had to think about that for a few seconds to realize it was true, and it made me laugh. Patsy was indeed the quintessential nerd: the smartest girl in our high school class, captain of the debate team, president of the chess club, valedictorian for the class of 1998. I have to admit I joined the debate team and the chess club just to be close to her. And the fact that she became my lab partner in Chemistry was, in my adolescent mind, the big trifecta. Of course I could never work up the courage to declare my feelings, or to ask her out on a date. I was just an acne-scarred, pimple-faced kid, praying that one day I could look in the mirror and not be mortified. When Mickey, who was a sophomore while we were seniors, asked Patsy to be his date for the Homecoming Dance, I could have strangled him. Didn't he know she was my dream girl?

We chatted for a while longer and then drifted back into the kitchen to refresh our drinks. That's when Gil Bradley, Mickey's best friend, came into the room carrying a very large box. He dropped it in the middle of the floor and we leaned in to take a look. Fireworks! Every variety of illegal fireworks you could imagine, piled to the top of that big box.

Gil looked around at all of us. "You know what Mickey would have done with this."

We looked at Gil and saw the tension in his face, the wild

look in his red-rimmed eyes. My brother Randy, Sheriff Randy McMillen, recently elected to a four-year term, looked into the box and shook his head.

"Is there anything in there that's legal?"

"Hell no!" Gil locked eyes with Randy. He didn't have to say it. He wanted Randy's permission to blow up this box of paper and gunpowder, to do it in honor of a guy he had loved since they were in kindergarten together.

Randy sighed and made his decision. "Okay, look. I'll give you cover through dispatch for one hour. Where are you going? How about down at the bridge where all the crap will fall into the water. Okay? One hour, that's it.

And with that we went tumbling out the kitchen door, piling into the nearest available vehicles for the race to the bridge.

The Koffee Kup was an institution in Millers Forge, a prairie town ninety miles from Kansas City. My parents bought the place twelve years ago, the year I graduated from high school. My mom served as general manager, cashier, and hostess. It was her business to run as she saw fit, and she'd done a fine job. The café was open for breakfast and lunch and the regular customers were there almost every day. It was a mini version of Times Square: if you stayed there long enough, everyone you knew in the county would walk through the front door.

My father's business, the Conoco station, was directly across Main Street. Dad had opened the station thirty-three years ago, just after my brother Randy was born. Millers Forge was the hub of the county and Dad drew his clientele not only from the townsfolk but from the surrounding farms as well. Most people filled their tanks at McMillan Conoco, but the real business was in the three service bays that were constantly busy with repair work. Dad built a reputation for quality service at a fair price, and he'd managed to keep up with the latest technology, purchasing state-of-the-art diagnostic equipment and training for his mechanics as cars and trucks became more and more like rolling computers.

I opened the door to the cafe and the bell attached to the doorframe rang brightly. It was just after 9:00 a.m. Mom was at the register and she greeted me with a tired smile. I'd always believed Margery McMillan was the prettiest mom in the entire county and I hated seeing her like this, her face so drawn. Like my dad, she'd never gained a pound, could probably still wear her prom dress, but now she looked very thin.

Mom really didn't need to be on the job the morning after Mickey's funeral, but there she was. She had insisted that being busy at work was better than sitting at home with nothing to do but think about Mickey. I gave her a hug and a kiss and asked her to join me when she had a few minutes to talk. There was an empty booth near the window that looked out onto Main Street. Mom brought two cups of coffee and slid into the seat across from me.

"How's it goin', Mom?"

"It's been pretty steady, honey. Just the usual crowd." She ran her fingers through her short dark hair, just now showing specks of gray.

"I wasn't referring to the café business. You know you could have taken a few days off." She glared at me. "Okay, okay. I won't mention it again." I paused for a few seconds before continuing. "It was a nice turnout for Mickey. The house was packed last night."

"Yes, well you know Mickey. He didn't have any enemies."

"True. Not even among the ex-girlfriends. I always envied his popularity. He made it look so easy."

She reached across the table and squeezed my hand. "I know it wasn't easy for you, Bart. But look at you now. Independent, successful, making a place for yourself in the world. You've done so well."

It took a few seconds for the lump in my throat to clear.

"Thank you, Mom. It's good to hear that from you. I wish I'd hear it from Dad."

"Look, Bart, your father is proud of you. Don't ever doubt it. The two of you just need to sit down and talk it out, put all the old hurt feelings behind you."

"I know—"

"He was hurt when you joined the Navy and went west, instead of coming into the business with him."

"It just wasn't for me, Mom. I needed to get out of this town, see more of the world for myself. I would have been miserable, and I'd have made you and Dad miserable too."

"Deep down he understands that, honey. You just have to give him a chance to come around. You need to start by talking to him, listening to him, give him a chance to listen to you."

"Yeah, I know—"

"And do it now, before you leave to go back to California. The two of you need to work this out."

I knew she was right. She'd always been the keeper of the family wisdom, the glue that held us together.

"I'll go across the street as soon as I have one of your delicious waffles. I'll make a date to sit down with him, away from the station, someplace where we can talk. Okay?"

She got up from the booth, hugged and kissed me, tears filling her tired eyes, and then headed back to her duties at the cash register. I waved to Donna, one of the waitresses who had worked at the Koffee Kup almost as long as my mom, and ordered my waffle.

Patsy and I had a date for later that day, a picnic lunch out at the lake. I would stop by and see Dad, set a time and place to have our talk, and then head home to get ready for the picnic.

—————✺✺✺—————

Patsy and I got as far as the parking lot for the beach area at the lake, and then I could go no farther. I was overwhelmed by the feeling that Mickey's death was so meaningless, that he'd lived and died for nothing, taken by a damn waterskiing accident in the prime of his life. And I was angry. How could he have been so reckless? There was no way I could sit on a picnic blanket looking out at the lake where my brother died. I just couldn't do it.

Patsy understood. We agreed to head back to the river, down below the bridge to the spot where we had gathered after the fireworks adventure. There was a sandy stretch along the bank and the river was clear and pretty this time of year.

Patsy had packed a nice lunch for us—bread and cheese, lots of fruit, fresh-baked cookies—and I'd brought a bottle of Chablis wrapped in a towel to keep it cold. We spread a blanket on the sand and dug into the lunch, talking quietly, bringing each other up to date on our lives.

She had earned her master's degree in education and was currently teaching English at the high school in town, our old alma mater. She was looking for a doctoral program, considering several possibilities, and eventually saw herself as a professor at the university level. Doctor Patricia Keller. It had a certain ring.

I told her about my progress in building a career as a software engineer. I'd had some success and landed a VP's position with a startup in San Francisco. Business was strong and growing and we were beginning to plan for an IPO. I'd fallen in love with Marin County and bought a house in Mill Valley, just north of the Golden Gate. I rambled on and on about Northern California, until I caught myself and apologized for boring her with the subject.

We walked down to the water's edge and I did my best to impress her with my ability to skip stones. Patsy skipped a few herself, every bit as impressive as mine, and I remembered that she was also a member of the varsity softball team back in the day. I wondered if there was anything she could not do.

Later, sitting on the blanket, she gave me a quick rundown on the people we'd gone to school with: the jocks, the cheerleaders, the student body officers, and of course, the rebels. I was amazed that it was so easy to talk to her now, remembering how tongue-tied I'd been when we were teenagers.

"You know, Patsy, I had a major crush on you. All through middle school and high school."

"I know. I liked you too."

"What? You're kidding me!" I was shocked. How could our signals have been so crossed?

"I kept waiting for you to make a move. I was a little too shy to make one of my own. When we were lab partners in Chemistry, I thought sure you'd ask me out."

"But, you went to the Homecoming Dance with Mickey. You know that broke my heart."

She smiled and laughed. "Talk about surprises. Mickey just walked up and asked me to the dance. I couldn't think of anything to say but 'yes.' You were the one I really wanted to go with."

We were sitting close together and I didn't have to move very far to kiss her—the first time. There were a lot of kisses after that and Patsy was very good at kissing, just as I had dreamed she would be. My heart pounded out of my chest and I wanted to shout *I love you! I've always loved you!* It was way too soon, but what a wonderful beginning.

The Koffee Kup was busy as usual, but I was able to secure that same booth next to the window. My dad had to open the station and make sure all the repair appointments were covered, and then he would join me. I sipped a cup of coffee and tried to organize my thoughts. It wasn't working. All I really wanted was for the two of us not to be angry anymore.

Out on Main Street, my dad stood on the corner, waiting to cross with the light. Henry McMillan was about five eleven, though he seemed taller. He'd never weighed more than a hundred and fifty pounds and he looked lean and neat in his khaki pants and shirt with the Conoco logo. His hair was cut in a short flattop style, last popular in the fifties, and at age sixty-five, it had gone gun-metal gray. I watched him cross the street and swing the door open, the bell ringing its happy tune as he came in.

My thoughts were still jumbled as he slid into the booth. Our waitress, a young girl I didn't know, brought coffee for my dad and menus for both of us, though we didn't need them. We both ordered waffles with eggs on the side and she smiled and hurried away toward the kitchen.

"Bart, I'm glad…you know—"

"Yeah, Dad, ah…I know you're…uh…busy." Shit. This was not going to be easy. It was quiet for a few seconds as we looked at each other across the table. There was a glint in his eye that I recognized. This was not going to go well.

"So, was that you and your friends, down at the bridge the other night, with the damn fireworks?"

Oh boy. He was pissed. We'd embarrassed him, created a rowdy scene on the day of his son's funeral. Now I was getting a little stirred up, too. I locked eyes with him.

"Yeah, Dad. That was us. Me and all of Mickey's friends."

"You couldn't wait?"

"Dad, come on—"

"You couldn't pick another night to go raise hell?"

"You got it wrong, Dad. It was like…like a tribute."

"Bullshit! Some tribute. And I can't believe you pulled Randy into it."

I was seeing red by then. I knew if I stayed in that booth, I'd say things I would regret later. I slid out without excusing myself and headed for the men's room near the front of the café. I locked the door, leaned against the sink, stared in the mirror, splashed water in my face—anything I could think of to calm myself, to make my heart stop racing. I'm not sure how long I was there, but someone began to jiggle the doorknob and knock. I unlocked the door, brushed past the man waiting outside, and started down the aisle toward the booth. My dad was not there. I turned toward the front of the café and caught my mom's eye. She gestured toward the front door. I looked out and saw Dad crossing Main Street, heading back toward the station.

——–⁓⚬⟋⚬⟋⚬⟋⚬⚬⁓⁓——–

I spent a beautiful Sunday with Randy and his brood. My sister-in-law Joanna did her magic in the kitchen while my brother and I watched my niece and nephew demonstrate their riding skills. Randy and Joanna had purchased eight acres out in the rolling country, enough to provide good grass for two ponies. Randy had built a corral and a small barn for the horses and he kept it well stocked with hay. Their rambling four bedroom house sat up on a knoll, the highest point on the property, and the view from their porch made me remember all the things I loved about home.

Their children, Randall Jr. and Dianna, ten and twelve years old respectively, were not sure what to make of Uncle Bart. It had been a long time since I'd seen them. Still they enjoyed showing off a little, first with the horses and then with a spirited game of soccer out on the front lawn.

Randy and I settled on the porch with a cold beer while the kids went to clean up for dinner. We were quiet for a minute, watching a trio of buzzards circling in the bright blue sky, a few puffy white clouds drifting through to the east. A white pick-up turned onto the road leading up the hill to the house. I looked at Randy, wondering who would be coming to visit. The truck came closer and I saw our parents in the cab, our father behind the wheel. I looked at Randy again.

"What the hell is this?" I started to stand up.

"Sit down, little brother. Yeah, this is a set up. You and Dad are going to talk. And then we are going to break bread. As a family, Bart. A family."

I knew better than to argue with my big brother. He could still break me in half if I made him angry enough. Mom and Dad climbed out of the truck and came up onto the porch. We got past the awkward greetings and Joanna miraculously appeared with a beer for Dad. Randy, Joanna, and Mom disappeared into the house and I was alone with Dad. My father wasn't one to waste time.

"Look, son, let's start over. Okay? Yeah, I was upset about the fireworks thing. But, yesterday I had a long talk with Gil Bradley. You know how close he and Mickey were."

"Yeah, I know. Since they were kids."

There was no glint in my father's eyes this time. They were red-rimmed and brimming.

"Gil told me the fireworks were, well, pretty special."

"They were spectacular!" I pronounced every syllable. "Mickey—"

"I know, son. Mickey would have loved it."

Dad's lower lip trembled. I should have grabbed him and hugged him right there, but we were never comfortable with open displays of affection. It took a few seconds to recover, but the ice had been broken. I opened my mouth and let it rip.

"Dad, I'm sorry things didn't work out the way you wanted. I know you wanted me to come into the business with you, but it just wasn't for me. I just had to get out of this town, not that there's anything wrong with Millers Forge. I just had to see what else was out there."

I waited then, searching his eyes, not knowing what to expect.

"You're right, Bart. I was counting on you to come in with me. I mean, we knew Randy only cared about law enforcement, about being a sheriff. That's all he ever wanted. And Mickey, well, Mickey was a damn fine mechanic, but he had no interest in running a business. That left you. Smart, good with numbers, good with people. I guess I saw you as a way to pass on my...my legacy. I know that sounds like a pompous ass thing to say, but that's how I felt. When you joined the Navy and went to California, I was hurt. I didn't take it well. And I took it out on you. I'm sorry."

I was surprised, but only for a moment. This was my dad: he'd always been a straight shooter. He never talked much, but when he did, he gave you the plain truth. But he wasn't finished.

"Okay, Bart...now what about you?"

"What do you mean?"

"I mean what about your side of this? You left home with barely a word. Came in one day and said you'd enlisted in the Navy. No discussion, didn't ask for advice. And then you were gone. I want to know—I think I *deserve* to know—why?"

He had me. There was no place to hide.

"Okay, here it is, Dad. When we were growing up, it was always you and Mickey. Playing catch in the driveway, or shooting baskets, or tossing a football around. You coached all his teams. You two were inseparable, and I was on the sidelines somewhere, watching. I wanted to be with you, too."

And now I'd said it out loud, no way to take it back. I'd been jealous of my little brother. My dad was quiet for a few seconds.

"Bart, it's true, Mickey was easy for me. We loved doing all the same things together. But you, well you always had your head in a book, and you didn't care about sports. I tried, I really did. I hung your straight-A report cards on the bulletin board at the station. I helped build your science projects and came to all the debate team events, even went to that chess match when you were a senior, which was like watching paint dry—"

"Are you listening to yourself, Dad? Don't you think I knew how you felt about the stuff I was interested in?"

It was quiet for a long time then. I wasn't sure what would come next.

"Bart, I hope you can see it from my side. I really did try. It just wasn't easy for me, like it was with Mickey. But think about this—you know how much I put into my business over the years, how hard I worked to make a go of it, through good times and bad. You know how much it means to me. And I wanted to leave it to you." He paused to let that thought sink in. "That's how much I respected you, son."

"Dad...I...I don't—" I honestly didn't know what to say. The word *respect* kept reverberating in my mind. My dad *respected* me.

Joanna opened the screen door. "Come on in, guys. Dinner is about to hit the table. Bart, I want to hear all about you and Patsy Keller, and don't spare the juicy details."

My niece and nephew swarmed around their grandfather to collect hugs and kisses as we headed in for dinner. I was amazed at Joanna's impeccable timing. Were they all listening from inside the house? It didn't matter.

A wall my father and I had spent years building was coming down.

———

"I should probably go." I glanced at the clock on the bedside table.

"Why don't you stay? This is nice, isn't it?"

"It's perfect."

"Yeah, it is."

"You were perfect. More than perfect, if there is such a thing."

She laughed. "You weren't too bad yourself, buck-o."

I paused for a few seconds. "My parents will be expecting me. They'll worry."

"So, call them."

"Yeah?"

"Yeah, tell them you're staying over."

"Okay."

"I'll get the phone for you." Patsy threw back the covers and walked quickly across the room to retrieve her cordless phone.

I watched her go and return and my body felt like I'd grabbed an electric fence. She was no rail-thin supermodel, not even close. She was a woman with a woman's lovely curves. She was beautiful. I couldn't wait to hold her again.

A while later, I dialed my parents' number and my dad answered. "Hi, Dad. Hey, just calling to let you know I won't be home tonight."

"Oh? You okay?"

"Yeah, I'm staying over at Patsy's. I'll see you guys in the morning."

"Okay, son. We'll have to leave around ten tomorrow morning to get you to the airport. Bart…" He paused for a moment. "Give Patsy our love."

I smiled and glanced at Patsy. "I will certainly do that. And, Dad…I love you." It felt clumsy when I said it, but I was determined to end every conversation that way from now on.

"Love you too, son."

Patsy smiled as I handed her the phone.

———

My flight left Kansas City right on time. I thought about closing my eyes and trying to sleep, but I knew it was useless. I was too jazzed to relax. Patsy would be coming to California next month for a visit and to check out doctoral programs at universities in the Bay Area. I couldn't wait to show her around Mill Valley, and San Francisco with its iconic bridges, hills, cable cars, and world-class restaurants. I knew she would love the wine country, and the Point Reyes Seashore, and maybe we could make it down to Monterey, or up to Lake Tahoe. Northern California has so much to offer, in addition to the great schools.

I'd also made plans to come home (yes, Millers Forge would always be home) for my dad's sixty-sixth birthday in October. It felt good to know that the two of us were on the right track, finally, after the lost years. And I was determined to make sure that he and Mom came west for a visit.

I glanced out the window at the thick cloud cover below the wings of the plane, a vast sea of cotton balls. Up ahead, I saw a break in the clouds and far below, somewhere on the prairie, a lake was coming into view. I thought about Mickey and felt my heart drop. How long would it be before I could look at a lake—any lake—and not think of my brother? As the scene below passed under the silver wing, I thought about my Dad and all the ground that we had gained. I thought about Patsy and our plans for the future. And I thought about how it all came together. I saw my reflection in the window, tears in my eyes, a smile on my face.

Look what you've done, Mickey. Just look what you've done.

Tool Six

from *Spitball*

A lex Wayne stood in the third base coaches' box and flashed the simple sign that said *hit away*. The batter, Denny Thornton, nodded and grinned. With the count two balls and no strikes and the bases loaded, the pitcher had to come in with a strike. No way would he risk walking in the go-ahead run, even if it meant pitching to the league's best hitter.

The pitch was on the outside corner at the knees, not a bad pitch at all. Denny dropped the bat head on the ball with his beautiful compact swing and drove it into deep right center. The ball clanged off the chain-link fence as the outfielders chased after it. All three base runners scored and the Valley Vista High Braves took a four to one lead. Denny stood on second base pumping his fist and soaking up the glory while six or seven scouts in the grandstand scribbled rapidly in notebooks and on scraps of paper. It was a familiar scene, one Alex had witnessed many times over the past three seasons.

The next batter popped out to short left field, ending the top of the seventh inning. Now the Braves needed just three more outs to clinch the league title. Alex looked around the dugout and then climbed the steps to scan the bleachers and the grandstand. Where the hell was Walker Bateman, the Braves head coach? He remembered seeing him leave the dugout after the top of the fourth inning, no doubt heading to the men's room to take a nip from the flask he carried. These absences were becoming more frequent and lasting longer. Alex had grown accustomed to taking over and managing the team until Coach Bateman resurfaced. He decided to let his pitcher, Teddy Sullivan, start the bottom of the seventh, but at the first sign of trouble he would have to make a change, with or without Bateman. A three run lead could evaporate in an instant in high school ball.

Damn, Walker. Where are you? Alex scanned the area again. *The league championship on the line and you take a powder.* It was a sad state of affairs for a man who was a legend in the high school coaching ranks. Walker Bateman had sent many players on to success at the college and pro levels. Now he was in his last season, sliding into retirement at age sixty-five. It was only the last few years—Alex tried to remember when, exactly—that Coach Bateman's drinking had gone off the rails. He'd always been known to enjoy a drink, but his wife Martha had managed to keep him in line. When he lost Martha, he lost control. His players, who once revered him and were proud to report they played for Walker Bateman, now referred to him (behind his back, of course) as W.B. It stood for whiskey breath.

The umpire called "play ball" and the bottom of the seventh got underway. Teddy Sullivan promptly walked the first batter on five pitches; he was running on fumes. Alex called time and walked slowly out to the mound. The infielders trotted in to join the meeting.

"Okay, Teddy. We're gonna make a change. You pitched a great game, son." Teddy handed Alex the ball. "Denny, I want you to close it out for us. Teddy, you'll go to shortstop." He handed the ball to Denny.

Denny Thornton lifted the ball above his head and looked toward the grandstand where his father was sitting next to the group of scouts. All eyes in the group around the mound turned toward Dennis Thornton Sr., "Big Denny" as he was known, who—after a dramatic pause—flashed a thumbs-up. The pitching change was approved and all the scouts scrambled to break out their radar guns.

"Okay, Coach. I got this." Denny flashed his cocky grin and got ready for his warm-up pitches.

The players trotted back to their positions and Alex headed for the dugout. *Geez, what if his old man said no? What then?* He had encountered obnoxious, intrusive dads before, but never anyone quite like Big Denny Thornton. The man was intent on reliving his glory days through his son.

Little Denny got the first hitter to pop up to second base and then struck out the next two with his low-nineties fastball. Game over and a league championship for the Braves!

The players celebrated around the mound and Alex let them enjoy the moment. Then he rallied them to line up and shake hands with their opponents. As he chatted with the opposing coaches, he could see Big Denny holding court with the scouts up in the grandstand, basking in his son's latest moment of triumph.

Alex directed the team to pack all the gear and load it onto the bus for the two-hour trip home. He assigned two of his seniors to make sure everyone got a sack lunch and a carton of milk, and then he turned his attention to finding Coach Bateman.

"Hey, Teddy." The player trotted to his side. "Do me a favor, hustle over to the men's room and see if Coach is in there."

"Yes, sir. No problem." Sullivan jogged away in the direction of the low concrete structure that housed the restrooms. He entered the men's room and a few seconds later, emerged and gave an urgent wave. Alex double-timed it across the grass to where Teddy was standing. "He's in the stall, Coach. I think he passed out."

"Okay, thanks. Go on back to the bus, and don't say anything. Okay?"

"Sure, Coach."

He knew it was pointless to ask the young man to conceal the situation. The team was well-aware of Walker Bateman's problem. Alex went into the men's room and bent down quickly to see that someone was, indeed, sitting in the stall. He banged on the door, loud enough to draw attention. "Coach? Coach Bateman? You okay in there?" No response. He repeated the pounding and called out again. Still no answer. Alex was worried now. He saw that the sink was situated next to the stall and that he could get a foot on it and hoist himself up to look over the partition. As he pulled himself up and looked down at the man sprawled across the toilet, Bateman's eyes snapped open.

"Jeezus! What the hell are you doin' up there?" He looked at Alex as if he were a crazy man—or a pervert.

"Game's over, Coach. Time to get on the bus and head for home."

"Well, hell. Did we win?"

"Yeah. Congratulations, Walker. Another league championship."

Bateman unlocked the stall door and walked out on shaky legs. He was tall and lean and his face was deeply tanned from too many hours in the sun.

"Are you going to be okay, to walk to the bus?" Alex resisted the urge to take his arm and steady his progress.

"Hell yes, I'm okay." He straightened his cap and adjusted his thick wire-rimmed glasses. "Did Sullivan finish the game?"

"No. I brought Thornton in to close."

"And his old man approved?"

"Yep. Gave us a big thumbs-up." Alex smiled.

"That son of a—"

"Come on, Walker. Let's go home."

And with that, they started across the grass to where the bus sat waiting at the curb, the engine running, the entire team watching their progress. Alex held great affection for this man who had been such an important part of his life. He felt a lump in his throat as they moved carefully toward the bus. It was the longest walk he could remember.

The bus rolled along the freeway heading north through the light traffic on a Tuesday evening. The sun was setting on this early-May day and Alex hurried to finish posting all the stats in the official scorebook before darkness fell. Walker Bateman leaned his head against the window and snored softly. Alex thought back to the years when he had played varsity ball for Coach Bateman. What a great experience that had been. In his mid-thirties now, Alex still maintained contact with many of his old teammates. They had taken great pride in wearing the Braves' uniform.

There were just two more games left in the season and then Coach Bateman would fade into the history of Valley Vista High, leaving behind a trophy case full of memories. Alex had been assured that he was in line to succeed his old coach and mentor. This had been his dream since coming onboard six seasons ago as assistant coach. He flexed his neck and shoulders and then reached back with his left hand to massage the knotted muscles. The stress of the game and finding the old man passed out in the men's room had taken its toll.

He thought about the handful of scouts at the game that day, guys he'd known for a long time, several of them going back to his playing days. How did they stand the constant travel, running around the countryside, everyone looking for the same thing? They all wanted a genuine, blue-chip, five-tool player; a kid who could run, throw, field, hit, and hit with power. Those elusive five tools!

You wouldn't think it would be that difficult to find, given the number of kids playing the game, and yet it was hard, damn hard. They generally settled for players missing one or more of the big five, hoping they would grow and develop power, or learn to hit the curve ball, or suddenly gain a step or two of foot speed. The search went on and on, looking for the next Mike Trout, or the next Bryce Harper.

Now the scouts were sure they had found their man and his name was Dennis Thornton Jr. No question about it, at six two, one hundred and eighty pounds and still growing, young Mr. Thornton was a five-tool guy. But in Alex's mind, a question mark remained. Would he become the next Mike Trout? Or would he squander his talent and opportunities on—what had Tug McGraw called it?—"wine, women, and bong"?

Alex closed the scorebook and tried to relax.

"Hey! Hey, knock it off back there!" The bus driver was staring intently at his rearview mirror, shouting to a group of players seated near the back of the bus. "Come on, you guys. Knock it off."

Alex spun around in his seat in time to see wadded-up lunch bags and milk cartons flying back and forth across the aisle. "Hey, you heard the man. Cut it out."

The trash continued to fly along with the laughter and shouted put-downs. Alex jumped up from his seat, the large scorebook still in his hand and strode toward the back of the bus. The trash fight stopped quickly.

"Look, you guys are going to pick up all this crap. Nobody gets off the bus until it's cleaned up. Got it?" Alex waited a few seconds and then turned around—just in time to be hit in the forehead by a tightly wadded lunch bag thrown by none other than Denny Thornton. The young man broke into his patented grin.

Alex drew the scorebook back with his right hand and slapped a hard backhand against the side of Denny's head. "You son of a bitch!"

It was dead quiet on the bus. The right side of Denny's face turned bright red. The grin was gone. "You callin' my mom a bitch, Coach?"

Alex froze for a moment, then turned to the young men seated around him, ignoring Denny Thornton. "You guys heard me. I want this mess picked up before we get off the bus."

He moved back down the aisle and took his seat behind the bus driver. He closed his eyes and tried to calm himself. *Oh my God! What have I done?* Coach Bateman continued to snore in the seat next to him.

―――――ⵘⵘⵘ⵿ⵘ⵿ⵘ⵿ⵘⵘ―――――

Alex sat in the coaches' office adjacent to the Men's Gym, waiting for his 7:15 AM appointment to arrive. Big Denny Thornton had called him at home and insisted on meeting first thing Wednesday morning. He was ten minutes late. At last the door pushed open and Thornton Sr. walked in. "Big Denny" was an appropriate tag for this man. He towered over Alex and he was built like an NFL lineman. His bald head glistened under the fluorescent lights. This was the first time Alex had seen him without a baseball cap. Thornton sat down in the chair on the other side of the desk. Neither man offered to shake hands.

"Good morning, Coach. How was your evening?" Thornton's voice dripped sarcasm.

"I think you know the answer, Mr. Thornton. Look, I am really sorry. I just lost my cool. Did Denny tell you everything that happened?"

"Well, yeah. Sounded to me like just a little horseplay. Ya know, boys will be boys." Big Denny smiled.

"Anyway, I am sorry, and I intend to speak to Denny and apologize face to face. I hope we can put this behind us."

"Yeah, I'm sure you do. You know, Alex, hitting a student-athlete is a pretty serious thing. Know what I mean?" He waited quietly, fully in charge now. "That sort of thing can cost you your coaching position, probably even your job. You have a wife, two little girls, a mortgage. This is not a good time for a teacher to be out of work. Am I right?"

Alex could feel the blood rushing to his cheeks. "Okay, Mr. Thornton. What is it that you want?"

Big Denny smiled again. "Well, now that you ask, the Major League Baseball draft is coming up in early June. My son, as I'm sure you know, is not college material. His dream, his best shot, is to be drafted by a major league team. If he goes high in the first round, the signing bonus will be pretty sweet. It's what we've been working for since I signed him up for T-ball."

"And? What do you want from me?"

"Scouts will be calling you, asking for your input. They don't want to talk to Walker anymore, they all know his situation. But they will listen to you, Alex. What you say can go a long way. Know what I mean?"

"And just what would you like me to say?"

Thornton opened a manila folder he'd carried in with him, removed a neatly printed sheet of paper and placed it in front of Alex. It was a bulleted list of talking points and, as Alex skimmed it quickly, it became clear that the purpose was to paint Dennis Thornton Jr. as a person of the highest character, a paragon of virtue. Regular church goer, Sunday school teacher, regular helper at the local rescue mission, volunteer for the suicide prevention hotline. The list went on.

Alex dropped the list on the desk and locked eyes with Big Denny. "Is any of this real?"

"Now, Coach, you know as well as I do that perception is reality."

"Yeah, well let me share my perception, from what I hear around campus. I hear your son likes to smoke a little weed while he enjoys a cold beer or two. And I hear he pays a couple of bright kids to write his papers for him. And then there's the big one, the girlfriend who was a little bit pregnant, which I'm told you paid to take care of. You want me to go on?"

Big Denny's smile was gone. "Now you listen to me, you little pissant!" He paused to regain composure. "You just keep this list handy when you talk to those scouts. And...nobody in the principal's office or the school district ever has to know *that you whacked my kid upside the head with your damn scorebook and called him a son of a bitch.*" He lowered his voice and continued. "Do we understand each other?" Alex did not respond. "All righty then. Thanks for your time, Coach. Let's stay in touch." He pushed back the chair, rose and left the office.

Alex stared at the piece of paper Thornton had left. So that was it. Just say all the right things when scouts called and life would continue apace. He could keep his teaching position, succeed Walker Bateman when he retired, and have a long and fruitful career at Valley Vista High.

It wouldn't be the first time he'd gone with the flow, or just turned his head. He'd been well aware of Denny's party boy behavior and his academic short cuts, yet never said a word. Hey, if the kid could throw shutouts and his batting average hovered around .450, why rock the boat? And what about Coach Bateman? Alex had gone along with the tacit agreement among the coaches to let Walker ease into retirement. And had he done enough to help the old man, other than an attempt to connect him with an AA sponsor?

The phone rang, startling him out of his stupor. It was Leo Haynes, head of scouting for the Chicago Cubs, one of the true gentlemen of the grand old game.

"Alex, my young friend. It's Leo Haynes. How the hell are you?"

"Just fine, Mr. Haynes. How's everything with you?"

"Top of the world, Alex, top of the world. And how is my old friend, Walker Bateman?"

"He's...well, I'm sure you know this. Walker has been better."

"Yes, that's what I've heard. Very sad. I have tremendous respect for that man. He is one of the giants. Please give him my best regards."

"I'll do that, sir."

"Listen, Alex, I don't want to take up too much of your time. I need to talk to you about young Denny Thornton."

Alex glanced down at the list on his desk. "Well, what can I say that you don't already know? He's the real deal, Mr. Haynes. A genuine five-tool player. There isn't a thing he can't do on a ballfield."

"Ah, yes, yes indeed. But that's not what I need to know. What is the young man like *off* the field? What kind of student is he? What kind of a citizen? Let me shuck it right down to the cob, Alex. If I convince the Cubs to spend a million or two to sign this young man, will I regret it? Is he likely to buy a Corvette and get arrested for driving a hundred miles an hour while under the influence? Is he likely to wind up punching out drunks in strip clubs? Or cold-cocking his girlfriend in full view of the security cameras, like whatshisname, the football player? I know all about the five tools, Alex. I need to know about Tool Six. Character! He either has it, or he does not. That's what I need to know."

And there it was, right to the point. Leo Haynes was living up to his impeccable reputation. Straight questions requiring straight answers.

"Mr. Haynes, listen, something urgent has come up. I'm going to have to call you back. Can I catch you around noon? Or maybe early afternoon?"

"Hmmm...okay, Alex. I'll look for your call around noon today." He gave Alex his mobile number and hung up.

Alex walked out of the office, down the hall, and out onto the quad that stretched from the Men's Gym to the stately Main Building. He watched the students coming and going, laughing and talking, on their way from one class to the next. Several of them called out to him with a cheery "Hi, Coach." He loved this old campus with its eclectic mix of buildings that ranged in style from classic Spanish-Moorish to the ultra-modern Science Building. From the day he decided to become a teacher, his dream had been to wind up right here at Valley Vista High. He was living his dream.

The sun in his eyes felt like God's flashlight. What had Leo Haynes called it? Tool Six? Haynes certainly had it. Walker Bateman had it too, in spite of his present condition. Alex thought back to his teenage years when it seemed he'd constantly been at war with his own father. Coach Bateman had always been there for him, counseling him to be patient and to see things from his father's point of view. Alex's dad did not understand the obsession with sports, or his desire to become a teacher. Dad's vision was of *Alex Wayne, M.D.*, or *Alex Wayne, Esq.*

He remembered Coach Bateman's words: "Be a scholar. Be a learned man. Whatever you choose to do, work hard and be the best you can be. Your father will be proud."

Alex took his cell phone from his pocket and dialed his wife's number at work.

"Hi, babe. How's it going?" Jill's voice was bright and positive, as usual.

"Oh, it goes." Alex could not match her upbeat mood.

"What did Big Denny want this morning?"

"Not much. Just a little blackmail."

"Really?"

"Yeah. I just need to tell the scouts that his son is a saint and no one will ever know about the incident on the bus."

They chatted a while longer, rehashing their discussion from the night before, a discussion that had extended into the early hours of the morning. Jill closed the conversation with conviction.

"Do what we agreed to, Alex. We'll get through this together."

Alex looked at the phone for a few seconds before he dropped it back into his pocket. He went back into the gym, down the hall and into the office. He paused to look at one of the framed pictures that covered the walls. It was the varsity baseball team from his senior year, 2001. In the yellowing photograph, Alex was standing in the back row, next to Walker Bateman. A hell of a lot had happened since that picture was taken, events that put his little dilemma into perspective.

It was 8:15 now. Hopefully the principal would be in his office. Alex looked at the phone on his desk. He picked up the handset and punched in the four-digit extension. Principal Albert Mullins answered on the second ring.

"Hello, this is Al Mullins."

"Good morning, sir. This is Alex Wayne."

"Hey, good morning, Alex. Congratulations on that league championship!"

"Thank you, sir." He took a quick breath and continued. "Sir, the reason I'm calling, I have something important to tell you, something you need to know. Can I stop by your office for a few minutes?"

"Oh uh, let me check my calendar."

Alex turned toward the picture on the wall as he waited. *Be the best you can be? I'm trying, Coach. I'm trying.*

THREE HUNDRED
SUNNY DAYS

Three hundred sunny days a year.
That's what my son Matt promised
when we discussed relocating from
Sacramento to Orange County.
During our first year, 2014, it was more
like three hundred and forty.
We had three seasons: sunny and warmer, sunny and cooler,
and partly cloudy with a chance of showers.
We could use more showers.

-C.W.S.

BEACH BOY BLUES

from *The Main Street Rag – Anthology, Fall 2017*

S loan walked in and took charge. No question about it, he was
The Man, The Boss, The Big Dog. He listened to a brief status
report from the early shift bartender and then set about doing his
thing: taking a quick inventory of the well, the cold case, the fruits
and veggies (as he called them), and making cryptic notes on a
small pad. He called Enrique over to the bar and sent him with the
list to replenish supplies. It was 11:15 and the lunch crowd would
begin to trickle in soon. Sloan didn't normally work the lunch shift
but a call from the general manager advising that the scheduled
bartender was "unavoidably detained" brought him hurrying the
few blocks from his house to the beachfront restaurant.

The Spindrift was a popular eatery and bar located in Laguna
Beach, California, with a multi-level deck that overlooked the
sand and the surf. With several well-maintained motels and hotels
nearby, the summer season always brought good crowds for the
breakfast buffet, then lunch and dinner, and the bar was generally
packed until closing time. Sloan ran the bar. His buddy Tony, an
accomplished chef, was in charge of the kitchen. Together they
made a good team. The general manager, Belinda, took care of the
accounting, the payroll, the hiring and firing, and making sure
the bar and the restaurant functioned as a well-oiled machine.

As Enrique hurried away to the storeroom, Sloan turned to
find Bobby, one of the waiters, ready to place an order.

"Hey, Sloan. How's it goin'? I need three Margaritas, two regular and one mango. All three blended."

"Got it. What's up, Bobby?"

"Not much. Hey, did you have a good time last night? Some party, eh? Could you believe the two brunettes in the pool?"

"No, man. What were they, twins or something?"

"Twins doin' that? Sisters? No way, dude! That would be sick."

"Yeah, well, I've seen worse…or better." He laughed at his own joke as he went about mixing the drinks, firing up the blenders, preparing the glasses.

"Hey, we may be goin' down there again tonight. Come along if you want."

"Thanks, but no. Vickie wasn't happy with me this morning. Know what I mean?"

Bobby laughed as he took the drinks on his tray. "Hey man, check out these *chicas* by the rail. I think they're into me."

Sloan watched as Bobby delivered the drinks and engaged in light-hearted banter with three attractive young ladies. Bobby would do well for himself here with his weightlifters' build, shaved arms and legs, dark hair combed into punky spikes, and those cool blue eyes. He fit the profile Belinda had established for the waiters this summer: hunky young guys to draw the beautiful young girls from up and down the beach, which in turn would draw more guys. Word gets around. Bobby, Cody, Allan, Jordan—they could pose for a calendar and it would sell like hotcakes. Or beefcakes.

Dalton, the unavoidably detained bartender, arrived and went to work. Sloan stayed on to help him through the lunch rush, at least until he could see that things were quieting down. He left Dalton in charge and walked over to the railing at the edge of the deck to scan the beach. The gray morning overcast had cleared away and the sun was shining in a bright blue sky. The surfers and the body boarders were out in force even though good waves were few and far between.

Sloan enjoyed the view for a while and then decided to head

for home and a nice afternoon nap. He was scheduled to be back for the evening shift and a little rest was in order, given the events of the night before. Vickie would be at work and he'd have the place to himself. On the way out, he stopped by the office to pick up his check from Belinda.

"Hi, Sloan. Ah, the eagle flies on Friday. Got your check right here. Though I still can't get used to seeing it made out to *Andrew Williams* and not *Sloan*. One of these days you'll have to explain that to me."

"It's simple." He laughed as she handed over his check. "Sloan is my stage name. Or I guess I should say it *was* my stage name."

"There must be a story behind it. An old family name? Your favorite hockey player? Something…anything?"

"Sorry to disappoint you, Belinda. Are you gonna be around tonight? Maybe I'll see you then."

In fact, there was a story behind his chosen name, but he'd never shared it with anyone. During his early days in L.A., when he was running around to auditions all over town, chasing any glimmer of an opportunity his agent could scare up, nobody seemed interested in an actor named Andrew Williams. Or Andy Williams. Too confusing. He wished he had a nickel for every time he was asked if he was related to the singer. His agent finally weighed in with fatherly advice: *Find a new name, kid. That is, if you want to work in this town.* So he ruminated and searched and read the phone book and filled pages in a notebook with possible monikers, but nothing seemed to fit.

One night he was out drinking with friends and made a visit to the men's room. As he unzipped his pants, he found himself staring down at a beautifully sculpted, modern water-free urinal, the manufacturer's name in bold print on the plastic disc covering the drain: SLOAN.

Yes, Sloan!

The well-known valve and fixture company was the maker of this fine product, but also a very cool, virile, manly sounding name, one you didn't hear every day. After this men's room epiphany, he became Sloan Williams. For a while, things picked up. He earned enough film credits for his SAG Card and toured with road companies for several Broadway shows. He even landed a couple of commercials, one of which went national. But it was all short-lived and before long he was back in the unemployment line, just another out-of-work actor in a town overflowing with them. He sought to hone his skills, joining local theater groups and earning roles—including several leads—in an endless string of productions. All of this was unpaid, of course. Waiting tables and tending bar paid the bills. And before he knew it, his twenties were gone, another decade had passed, and he was staring in the face of the Big Four-0h.

Then his friend Tony, another former actor, told him about the job at the Spindrift. Tony had found a way to go to culinary school and had become a highly sought-after chef. He recommended Sloan for an opening on the wait staff and the rest, as they say, is history. Sloan set his acting dream aside and after a lot of hustling and hard work, he took over behind the bar. He discovered that he had a talent for running a saloon, for building a solid team, for keeping all the players—or most of them—on the same page, all the while enhancing the bottom line.

At the Spindrift bar, Sloan Williams was The Man.

He headed for home, up the hill and across Pacific Coast Highway, then two more blocks to the cottage he shared with Vickie. It was a great little place with an ocean view and he was lucky to find it. He had advertised for a roommate, someone to share the rent and fill the second bedroom, and Vickie answered the ad. Victoria Mattison was a stunning redhead, five years his junior, and she turned heads whenever she entered a room. She was also a successful mortgage broker in the lucrative Orange County market. Vickie transitioned from roommate, to best friend, to lover, and the second bedroom became a storage room, a place to stash all their spare things.

Sloan's friends were unanimous on the subject of Vickie Mattison: "Dude, she's the best thing that's ever happened to you, and don't forget it."

Before he could turn the key and open the old-fashioned French door, he saw the note taped to the inside of the glass. It was from Vickie.

"I'm going to stay with Stacy for a few days. Don't call me, Sloan. I need some space to sort things out." She closed with her typical sarcastic wit. "In the meantime, you might think about growing up."

He closed the door and turned to look down the hill toward the beach and the ocean beyond, where six or seven surfers floated on their boards, waiting for the perfect wave. He knew Vickie was right, but what incredible timing. Tomorrow was his birthday.

Sloan went to the bedroom, stripped to his boxers, and from there to the bathroom to brush his teeth, focused now on that all important afternoon nap. As he rinsed his mouth and dried his face, he took a long look in the mirror. He saw a guy who had aged pretty well, given the hard living he'd done. There were dark circles under his eyes, but that was a carryover from last night. The nap would fix it. There was just a touch of gray creeping into his temples and if it started to spread through his thick dark hair, a little Just For Men would take care of it. He was lean and well built, thanks to his work with the barbells in the second bedroom, not to mention the one hundred crunches he did most days.

In spite of his positive assessment, he could see it coming, like a bullet train through a mountain tunnel: the crow's feet around his eyes, the deepening furrows in his brow. And were his ear lobes getting longer, or was he imagining? There was no denying that he was aging, looking every bit of his thirty-nine years, three hundred and sixty-four days. He made a promise to himself as he stood there leaning over the sink: healthier food, less booze, no more recreational drugs, more exercise, sunblock every day after he shaved, plus a nice Panama hat to wear when he planned to be out in the sun. In other words, all the things that would have made Vickie happy, or at least happier. He surprised himself by speaking out loud to his mirror image.

"You really blew it, buddy boy. You blew it big time."

———⁓꘎꧁ꦙꦙ꧂꘎⁓———

Sloan heard the murmur run through the crowd and glanced up to see every head at the bar turned toward the wooden walkway that was the entrance to the deck. He recognized her right away, in spite of the floppy sunhat and the oversized amber sunglasses that seemed to hide much of her face. Dressed in platform sandals, white slacks and a silky black top that let one alluring shoulder peek out, it was clear that she was *somebody*. It was Mallory Goodhue, star of stage, screen, television, and probably radio. Her career had been a long one, filled with ups and downs, periods when it seemed she had disappeared, only to see her rebound into the spotlight. Her latest feat was a hit sitcom that had been picked up for a second season based on promising ratings. She played the matriarch of a hilariously dysfunctional family, an altogether appropriate role for an actress in her early sixties.

She took a seat at the corner of the bar and placed her hat on the stool next to her, a gesture that said *don't even think about sitting here.* Sloan moved toward her with a warm smile.

"Welcome to the Spindrift, Miss Goodhue. What can I get for you?"

"Oh my...well...that lovely welcome will do for openers." She flashed a brilliant smile in return. "I will have a very dry Beefeater martini, stirred not shaken, mustn't bruise the vermouth, with two of those heavenly stuffed green olives."

"Excellent!" He hurried about mixing the drink, taking a light hand with the vermouth. He slid the martini in front of her with a flourish. "There, my lady, taste that. And if it's not perfect, I'll try again."

She lifted the long-stemmed glass and brought it to her lips. "Well well well, nicely done, smiling young man. A winner right off the bat."

He couldn't resist adding a comment while he had her attention. "By the way, I love your show. I hear it's been picked up for another twenty-two episodes. Congratulations! Here's to a long, successful run."

"Aren't you the sweetest thing! Can I buy you a drink? You *are* starting a tab for me, are you not? I'm meeting someone here and a late arrival would not surprise me."

"Yes and yes. It will be a pleasure to lift a glass with you."

Sloan quickly mixed a drink for himself, the one he called Wally's Curse. Years ago he'd worked with a veteran bartender who would scoop ice cubes into an Old Fashion glass, toss in a generous shot of vodka, add a splash of orange juice, and then drink it down in one or two gulps. By the end of his shift, Wally was lucky to be on his feet. Poor guy never lived to collect Social Security. Sloan touched glasses with Mallory, finished Wally's Curse in one swallow, and then moved down the bar to serve other customers.

It was after 9:30 p.m. and the restaurant crowd was beginning to clear out. Before long the late-night partiers would shuffle in. As the evening wore on, Sloan mixed several more martinis, and a few more Wally's. Mallory sipped her drinks slowly, munching happily on the large green olives. Now and then a customer would work up the courage to approach her and engage in the usual star-struck chatter. She handled this with style and grace, and Sloan was impressed. When there were lulls in the action at the bar, he would wander over to chat, telling her about his abandoned acting career, sharing a few war stories. But he saved his best story for a long quiet period.

"You know, I was in a play with you once, about twelve years ago. You were touring with a revival of *A Streetcar Named Desire*. I joined the company in L.A., at the Ahmanson."

"Oh my God! You're kidding me. What did you say your name was? And what was your role?"

She showed little effect from the martinis. Her speech was clear and she sat ramrod straight on her stool. The only impact he could detect was in her eyes which had lowered to half-mast.

"Sloan Williams. I was an understudy for several roles, but primarily for the boy who comes to collect for the newspaper."

"I don't believe this. How intriguing. Did we ever perform together?"

"No. Unfortunately the guy I was understudying was a real trooper. Never missed a show."

"Oh, how unfortunate. If we had performed together we would have kissed. Truly a missed opportunity." She was smiling and laughing now, flirting openly, enjoying herself. She went into character and spoke the famous line: "'I want to kiss you, just once, tenderly and sweetly on your mouth.'"

"I have to say that watching you do Blanche DuBois night after night is one of my best memories. You seemed to bring something new to every performance...and twice on Sunday." Sloan meant every word. Her portrayal of Blanche was without doubt his favorite, including Vivien Leigh's Oscar-winning performance in the movie version.

Time passed and it became clear that Mallory's date was not going to show. She asked if there was a phone she could use to call a car service for a ride back to Beverly Hills. Her cell phone battery had gone dead. Sloan helped her to Belinda's office, her legs wobbling a little, but before she could make the call, she spotted the comfortable leather couch against the wall. She let out a dramatic sigh, kicked off her shoes and plopped down, her magnificent array of blonde hair spread over a throw pillow.

"Please turn out the lights, dear Sloan. And call me in an hour or two."

With that she closed her eyes and drifted away, a contented smile on her famous face. Sloan did as she asked, checking his watch and noting that closing time would arrive in sync with her requested wake-up call.

———ᴡᴏᴏᴇᴏᴏᴋᴇᴏᴏᴡᴡ———

His eyes blinked open and for a few seconds he wasn't certain of what was real. Was he dreaming? No, he was awake. He tried to judge the time by the light that was filtering in through the blinds and he guessed that it was around 8:00 a.m., maybe 8:30. He turned his head on the pillow and there she was, her back turned toward him, sound asleep. It was not a dream. It actually happened. He pulled back the covers and retrieved his boxers from the floor, found his jeans and a T-shirt, and made his way to the bathroom. From there he went to the kitchen and in a minute or two, the coffee maker gurgled, the strong, dark liquid collected in the pot, and the aroma spread to fill the room. He fumbled through one of the cabinets, found a bottle of aspirin, and swallowed three in one gulp with a little water. He remembered now that Wally's Curse came with a serious hangover. With a cup of steaming coffee in hand he went to the window and opened the blinds. A thick marine layer obscured the view, likely to hang on until midday or longer. He began to play back the events of the night before.

After closing the bar, he went to Belinda's office to wake Mallory. He found her sitting up, wide awake and refreshed by her nap.

"Oh, dear Sloan, thank you for taking care of me. I fear it's too late for my car service."

"Probably true. Well then, you'll just have to come home with me. I live right up the hill. A short walk in the cool ocean air will do us good, don't you think?"

She resisted for a minute or two, but then agreed to be his guest. He offered his arm and as she stood up to take it, she couldn't resist slipping back into character.

"'Whoever you are—I have always depended on the kindness of strangers.'"

They ran into Tony on the way out and he offered them a ride. They decided that the cool ocean air was overrated and accepted his offer. The kissing, the touching, the fooling around, started while Tony went to retrieve his car. It continued in the back seat on the short ride up the hill. When they arrived at the cozy little cottage, Mallory took charge and directed their love scene. She knew exactly what she wanted and he did his best to follow direction, amazed that she was so firm and athletic. But it was the pillow talk afterward that stunned him and had him shaking his head in disbelief.

"You know, dear Sloan—I simply adore that name!—we are going to be casting an actor for a recurring role on the show. One of our leads has had a falling out with the producers and they want to bring in a new character, a way of demonstrating that he can be replaced."

"Okay...so?"

"So, I think you would be perfect for the part. Absolutely perfect!"

"Come on, Mallory. Don't mess with me. That would be cruel."

"I am completely serious, darling Sloan. And believe me, I can make this happen."

He could not believe it, at least not right away. Mallory finally convinced him. She could see to it that he became the new recurring character on her hit sitcom. The possibility thrilled him. The show appeared to have legs, the critics adored it, the writing was the best of the season just concluded, and if the quality of the scripts could be maintained, it looked like a good long run. It would only take five or six seasons to put the show into syndication and then everybody involved would live happily ever after. Look at *Friends*. Look at *Everybody Loves Raymond*. Look at *The Big Bang Theory*, for God's sake. After all the years of struggling, of fighting for that break that never came, suddenly

Mallory Goodhue walks into his life and *Wham*. The classic line from *Casablanca* leapt into Sloan's mind: "Of all the gin joints, in all the towns, in all the world, she walks into mine." It was a good fit, even though the context was wrong.

It was a little past 9:00 a.m. now and Sloan decided that breakfast was in order for his guest. He checked the refrigerator and found eggs and some packaged cheese. He had a few tomatoes and an onion. Just enough groceries for a couple of omelets. There was even half a loaf of bread for toast.

He decided to check on Mallory and see if she was awake. He opened the door to the bedroom and saw that she hadn't moved. He walked over and rubbed her shoulder gently. No movement. Then he shook her, several times, with increasing urgency. Still nothing. Oh my God. Was she okay? Had something happened? He watched to see if she was breathing. Was there any movement? He took her wrist and felt for a pulse but didn't know what he was doing. He couldn't be sure. His mind was racing, trying to stave off panic. What was that lemon-yellow pill she had offered him, promising it would *enhance the experience*? Thank God he'd refused. Had she OD'd right there in his bedroom? Sloan hurried into the bathroom and found a small hand mirror, then back to the bed to hold it under her nose, hoping—no, praying!—to see fog forming on the glass. Nothing. At least nothing he could detect. Oh God oh God oh God no no no. This could not be happening, not now. He ran back into the kitchen and leaned hard against the sink, afraid he would be sick. He had to do something, but what? Load her into his car and rush to the nearest hospital? Call 911? Call a friend, call Tony, anyone who could help him think his way through this shit storm? One last desperate thought ran through his mind: grab the car keys and get the hell out of Dodge. But to where? And how could he explain a dead celebrity in his bed? There was the telephone, sitting on the counter. There was no way out. He would have to call 911.

Sloan started across the room to the phone. And then he

heard it, strong and clear from the bedroom: a very long, loud, melodious fart, followed by an equally loud moan. Oh thank God thank God thank God! She was alive. He went to the bedroom door and pushed it open. Mallory was sitting on the side of the bed, clutching the sheet around her torso.

"My God, Sloan darling, what time is it? Why didn't you wake me?"

Sloan could not answer. He was busy wiping his eyes with the sleeve of his T-shirt. He finally found his voice. "Are you okay? I mean...you *are* okay, aren't you?"

"My head is splitting open. Do you by chance have any Advil or some such? I'll take anything you have."

He hurried away to fetch aspirin and water. When he returned, she was up with the sheet still wrapped around her, his cordless phone pressed to her ear. She ended her call and thanked him for the aspirin.

"How about some coffee? I can make you an omelet. Are you hungry?"

"Some coffee and dry toast would be wonderful, dear Sloan. I must take a shower. Where do you keep your towels?"

He handed her two towels from the hall cabinet and she disappeared into the bathroom. A second later, the water was running and he could hear her singing softly. He went into the kitchen and as he dropped two slices of bread into the toaster, a key rattled in the front door lock. Sloan looked up to see Vickie coming through the door, a pink cake box in her hand. She smiled at him and began to sing.

"*Happy Birthday to you / Happy Birthday to you / Happy Birthday, dear Sloan / Happy Birthday to you.* Hello, Birthday Boy. What? Did you forget? It's your Big Four-Oh. Forty years old today. You didn't think *I'd* forget did you?"

Vickie walked toward him, holding the cake box, her beautiful red hair cascading around her shoulders. She placed the box on the counter, untied the string, and lifted out a chocolate cake inscribed with "Happy Birthday, Sloan" in pink script. Then she heard singing, coming from the bathroom. The door opened and Mallory emerged wrapped in a towel, a second one wound around her head to dry her hair.

"Sloan, darling, would you please...oh hello...sorry to interrupt. Don't mind me. I'm just going to get dressed and I'll be out of here. I called the car service and they are on the way. I'll have to take a rain check on the coffee and toast." She hurried into the bedroom and closed the door.

Vickie stared at the door, and then she turned to Sloan.

"Holy crap, Sloan! I wasn't even gone for a whole day."

"Come on, Vickie, don't jump—"

"Is that who I think it is? Mallory Goodhue?"

"Yeah."

"So you traded up? Is that it?"

"Vickie, you don't understand, let me explain—"

"Okay, I'm listening. And this better be good."

Sweat collected on Sloan's upper lip. "It's just that...you know...I mean—"

"Oh for God's sake. Save your breath, dickhead! You really can't help yourself, can you? Forever the naughty little boy." She headed out the front door, leaving it wide open. "Enjoy your fucking cake."

Mallory came out of the bedroom, smiling her brilliant smile. "Maybe I will have that coffee, dear Sloan. And did you say you had some toast for me? Oh my, what a lovely cake." She didn't bother to read the inscription. "And who was that perfectly gorgeous redhead?"

"Oh, uh...that was Vickie. She...she lives here."

"Of course. There's always a Vickie, isn't there. That would explain some of the products in your bathroom, and the chic wardrobe hanging in the closet."

There was a knock at the open door and a young man in a black suit stuck his head in. "Car service?"

"Yes, oh thank you for being so prompt. I'll be right out." Mallory turned to Sloan and put her hands on his shoulders, peering into his eyes. "Thank you, Sloan darling, for everything. You've been a dear."

"Yeah, a real prince. Listen, Mallory, about the role in your show that we talked about…"

"Role, darling? I'm not sure what you mean."

"The new recurring role that you're casting."

"I'm not following you. But listen," she said, digging into her purse, "here is my card. Call this number and my representative will be happy to help you. And now I really must run. Goodbye, dear Sloan." She gave him a quick air kiss that almost touched his cheek.

Mallory left with a flourish and slid gracefully into the limo as the young man in black held the door. The driver gave Sloan a smile and a salute as he rounded the front of the car. The big black sedan rolled slowly away, taking with it Sloan's last ounce of hope.

"Well," he said, to no one in particular, "at least there's fucking cake."

Imperfect Game

G rant was dumbstruck. He almost dropped his bottle of beer, which would have been a shame because it was fresh and full and very cold. Gwen walked toward him, a pleasant smile on her face, short blonde hair bouncing, blue eyes flashing. She was an attractive woman, perhaps a few pounds overweight, not bad for a mother of two pre-teens.

"Hi, Grant! I didn't know you bowled on Monday nights. Good to see you."

She held out her hand, a rather awkward gesture, which Grant accepted with a gentle shake. They'd met several months earlier at an office party and he recalled a brief conversation. Thank God he remembered her name.

"Hi, Gwen. Good to see you too. Yeah, Monday is the traditional night for our company team. Our league has been here at Saddleback Lanes for about five years."

"Tuesday was always the night for our league up in Lake Forest, but we got switched this year to Mondays at Saddleback. Anyway...how's it going?"

"Oh, we're gettin' our butts kicked tonight." Grant laughed and gestured toward the scores projected on the overhead screen. "How about you?"

"Yeah...about the same. But I wasn't asking about bowling. I meant how are things with you and Tracey?"

One of Grant's teammates called to him. It was his turn on

the right-hand lane. "Oh…excuse me, Gwen, I'm up. I'll catch you later."

"Yeah, I've got to get back too." She smiled and waved.

Grant was more than a little rattled. How the hell had this happened, winding up bowling on the same night as the wife of his estranged wife's boyfriend? *Boyfriend, my ass. Let's tell it like it is—my wife's lover. Geez…how much does she know? She walks up all open and friendly. She's probably still in the frickin' dark, totally clueless.* Grant's mind was a jumble and his first ball nearly wound up in the gutter, missing the headpin completely, leaving a nasty washout. He waited near the ball return, drying his hand over the blower. His hand was shaking.

Larry, his teammate and best friend, approached and clapped a hand on his shoulder. "Hey, man, what's up with that? You nearly put that one in the ditch. We're still in this, dude. We can pull this game out. Get some focus here and pick up the spare, okay?"

"Yeah, Larry. My bad. I got this one."

Grant didn't have it. He managed to chop a couple of pins and wound up with an eight-count and an open frame. His teammates needled him a little, called him a wimp and had some fun at his expense, then came to him one by one to tell him to get it together. Larry, John, Gene, and Cal—they were competitors. No one liked losing.

They were well into the third game of the three-game series when Gwen approached again. Grant met her on the gallery level behind the lanes. He didn't want his teammates to overhear the conversation. Gwen had a question for him and she got right to it.

"So, Grant, I know that Rod is over at your place all the time. Don't you and Tracey get tired of him hanging around?"

Shit! There it is. She doesn't know what's going on, doesn't know I moved out a couple of months ago. Damn, what am I going to say? Better play it safe. "Ha! No…it's no problem. He's always welcome. We enjoy his company." He paused a moment, then blundered ahead. "Hey, you should come along, bring the kids.

Our boys would love it. The kids are about the same age, right?"
*Oh, God. I've put my foot in it now. I'd better tap dance out of this
conversation in a hurry.* "Oh, I'm up again, Gwen. Nice talking to
you. See you next Monday...if not before."

Grant forced a smile and headed back to the lanes. He glanced
up and saw that Gwen was still standing there, a quizzical look on
her face. He picked up his ball and stepped out on the approach.
Okay, dummy, concentrate, focus, you need a mark in this frame.
His foot stuck at the line as he delivered the ball and he hopped
forward tripping the foul light. *Damn!* The situation was going
from bad to worse.

——— ᴡᴡᴏᴏᴇᴛᴏᴏᴛᴏᴏᴏᴡᴡ ———

Grant was at his desk early Tuesday morning. He waited until
a few minutes after 8:00 a.m. to dial his wife's number at work.
Tracey answered on the third ring.

"Newport Financial Services, how may I help you?"

"It's Grant, Tracey. Have you got a few minutes? We need to
talk."

"Yeah, okay. Let me close the door." She was gone for a few
seconds. "So...what's up?" Her tone was cool and distant.

"Did you know that Gwen bowls on Monday night, at the same
place as my company team?"

"What? No...I didn't know."

"She came over and chatted with me a couple of times, asked
me if we were tired of having Rod hang out at our place so often.
Tracey, she doesn't know we're separated. I thought Rod was going
to talk to her, come clean, tell her what's up with the two of you."

"He *is* going to tell her. He just can't do it right now. She's
unstable, she might...she might do something drastic, something
stupid...she might hurt herself."

Tracey's tone had changed. Grant could tell she was fighting
for composure. He was torn between compassion and anger, and

anger was winning. He could picture his hands around Rod's throat, his fist smashing into his swarthy face. *Man up, you sonofabitch! Tell your wife what's going on!* He took a deep breath and tried to be calm.

"Look, Tracey, it's likely I'm going to see Gwen every Monday night for the entire season. I'm not going to keep up this charade forever. I'm not going to keep lying to protect you and Rod."

"Are you threatening me, Grant? Don't you *dare* tell her anything. If you do, I'll never speak to you again…as long as I live." The battle for composure was lost. Tracey's sobs were loud and clear.

"I'm not threatening you, Tracey. I'm just stating a fact. I can't keep up this lie forever. You and Rod need to get it together. Soon!"

The phone call was over, ending in anger and tears like so many conversations before. It was hard to tell who hung up first. There were no goodbyes, that much was certain.

———⁓⁓∿⊙⊙⊹⊙⊙∿⁓⁓———

Saddleback Lanes in Mission Viejo was a short drive from Grant's apartment. He cruised along Oso Parkway, the frozen dinner he'd wolfed down still churning in his stomach. He wasn't sure what to expect this Monday night. Maybe Gwen would take a week off, let a substitute fill in, and he wouldn't have to evade her questions, or look her straight in the eye and lie. The more he thought about it, the angrier he became.

They were into the middle of the first game when he saw her walking his way. He went up to the gallery level to meet her.

"Hey, how's it going? Better than last week I hope." She had a nice smile, and she looked cute in her bowling shirt with the company logo stitched on the breast.

Grant laughed. "Yeah, well not much better, so far. The night is young. Magic can still happen." He listened while she told a story about something one of her kids had said, something profound for a nine year-old, though it went through his mind and didn't stick. It was good that she didn't expect him to respond, other than to smile and laugh at the right moments. His thoughts were elsewhere. Grant had been formulating a plan. *What the hell. I'm gonna do it. Why frickin' not?*

"Gwen, how about joining me for a quick drink or a cup of coffee, when we're finished bowling? Do you have a little time? Don't want to hold you up if you're in a hurry to get home."

Gwen paused and looked at him for a moment. "Okay...sure. I'll meet you in the lounge. We'll probably finish about the same time, right?"

"Yeah, sure, I'll see you then."

Grant headed back to join his team, his mind spinning, hashing out the details of his plan. Larry sat down next to him between frames.

"Grant, who is the blonde you've been chatting-up? Kind of a cutie, eh?"

"Yeah, you won't believe this, Larry. She is Rod's wife."

"Wait a minute. You mean Rod, the guy who's with your wife?" Grant had shared the details of the demise of his marriage and his wife's affair.

"Ain't but one."

"Holy shit! Well, the two of you have some interesting things to talk about, that's for damn sure."

"Depends on your point of view. She doesn't know about Tracey and dear Rodney. The poor kid has been treated like a mushroom, kept in the dark and fed bullshit."

"So what are you talking to her about?"

"I'm just gonna give her some advice. Something to spice up her love life."

Larry stood up. It was his turn on the lanes. "Sounds dicey, Grant. Better watch yourself."

The lounge at Saddleback was a throwback to an earlier era, lots of faux stone and dark paneling. Ornate sconces on the wall provided the dim light. They found two empty stools at the bar, Grant ordered a beer—at least one more than he needed—and Gwen a cup of decaf coffee.

"Glad you could join me, Gwen. I thought it would be easier to talk here and not be interrupted by rushing off to bowl."

"Thanks, Grant. I can't stay long. The alarm goes off at the same time, bowling or no bowling."

"I can't stay either. Tracey waits up for me. I don't like to keep her waiting." He made his best attempt at a wry smile.

"She waits up for you? Past midnight?"

"Oh yeah. There's something about me being out with the boys, doing guy things. It turns her on." Grant laughed and smiled again. "How about Rod? Is he *up* for you?" He tried not to sound too suggestive.

Gwen smiled, then looked away. "No…not lately. He's usually sound asleep."

"Well I'm sure he'd appreciate it if you woke him up, maybe in a special way." Grant was grinning at her now and though the light was dim, he could see the blush on her pale cheeks. Had he planted the seed? She gave him an embarrassed smile.

———⁓⁓⊙⊙⊙⊙⊙⁓⁓———

It was 7:58 a.m. when Grant's office phone began to ring. It was Tracey and she was furious.

"What in the hell are you doing?"

"Whoa…wait a minute. Mind telling me what you're talking about?" Grant couldn't suppress a smile.

"You know exactly what I'm talking about. Did you tell Gwen that I wait up for you on Monday nights, to have sex? That I get 'turned on' by you being out with the guys?"

"Sounds familiar. I may have said something like that. Is it a problem? It plays right into your charade that I'm still living at home."

"You are messing with my life, Grant, and you need to stop it. Now!"

"How is this messing with your life?" He tried to sound innocent.

"You know damn well. Gwen comes home and puts these big romantic moves on Rod, practically rapes him—"

"Oh my goodness!" Grant was laughing now. "Are you saying Rodney is being seduced by his wife?"

"You bastard! Just stop what you're doing. And I mean right now!"

There was a loud click as Tracey slammed down her phone. Grant placed his handset gently in the cradle, sat back in his chair, and smiled. Larry came into his office and dropped a report on his desk.

"Hey, buddy. What's goin' on? You look pleased with yourself." Larry plopped down in a chair in front of the desk.

"That was Tracey. She's pissed because Rod's wife is hot for his bod, warm for his form…" Grant searched for another cliché but couldn't find one. "It seems my suggestion to Gwen took root."

Larry paused for a moment, staring at his friend. "Are you sure you want to play this game, Grant? You know, it's a game nobody wins. It's one thing for you to cause trouble for Tracey and Rod. It's something else altogether for you to use Gwen like a tool. She's a person. She has feelings too."

Grant had no answer, at least not a rational one. "Hey, I'm not… Gwen can take care of…They deserve..." He paused, reaching now for justification. "Let me tell you the latest. I asked Tracey what she saw in Rod, what was so great about him. She tells me that for one thing, he has this very strong sense of right and wrong. I ask, 'how so?' She says he was over at our house one day and she suggested taking a bike ride. Tracey and I have two nice ten-speeds in the garage. Rod says, 'No, I can't do that. That would be wrong. That's

Grant's bike.' And she sees *this* as his big sense of right and wrong. I mean come on! He won't ride my bike but he'll sleep with my wife? Give me a freakin' break!"

Larry looked away for a moment. He turned to lock eyes with Grant. "Dude, are you listening to yourself? That little story, as outrageous as it is, has nothing to do with Gwen. Don't you see that? When the shit hits the fan, and it will, it's going to blow right in her face. You're just adding to the pile. Does she deserve that?" He stood and started for the door. "I'm going to get some coffee. See you later, pal."

Grant watched him walk away, heading down the hall toward the breakroom.

———————

It was nearing midnight when Grant and Gwen took their customary stools at the bar. They had been meeting like this for several weeks. Grant had bowled miserably again and his mood was foul, tinged with meanness. They talked about nothing in particular for a while, then Grant swung the conversation in a new direction.

"So, Gwen, how's Rod? He hasn't been over for a while." He knew that wasn't true. It would provoke a response.

"Oh really? Seems like he's there all the time." She gave him a puzzled look.

Grant glanced at his watch. "Oh, man. Later than I thought. I'd better finish this and get home to Tracey. The girl can't wait, know what I mean?"

"Ha! Good for you, Grant."

"How's it going with you and Rod? Did you take my suggestion?"

Gwen smiled and looked away. "Yes I did. And it worked fine, for a while. But it's getting harder to wake him up now."

Grant's mind seethed. *That sonofabitch! He's got* his *wife and* mine *too*. He took a long drink from his beer and decided to forge ahead.

"You know, you should try what Tracey does. I guarantee he'll wake up…very happy, as a matter of fact."

"Really? What's that?" Gwen was genuinely interested, almost desperate to hear.

"It's a little embarrassing to talk about."

"Come on, Grant, tell me."

"Well, okay…" He cupped his hand and whispered in her ear.

"Oh my God!" Gwen looked away, her cheeks flushed.

Grant smiled. *There you go, Rodney old pal. You can thank me later.*

They finished their beverages and headed for the parking lot.

Grant signaled the bartender for another round and continued his story, his friend Larry playing the role of *good listener*.

"So, Tracey asked me if I'd think about coming home. 'Think' about it." Grant's speech was beginning to slur.

"And what did you say?"

"I said, 'Hell yes. You know I'll be there, just say the word.'"

"So, that's good. Right?"

"Shit no. She'll tell Rod, 'Grant is thinking about it.' That'll light a fire under his ass. This ain't the first time she's asked me to 'think about it.'"

"Look, Grant, I know you want to get back with Tracey, back with your kids. But look what you're doing with Gwen. Do you think that's going to help?"

Grant ignored the question. "Maybe I should shoot that sonofabitch. Just plug dear Rodney right between the eyes. I could hide in the weeds in the field across the street, blow his brains out as he's comin' out my front door."

"Yeah, and wind up in prison for the rest of your life. Don't even joke about it. That's just jealousy talking."

"What makes you think I'm joking?" Grant turned to stare at Larry.

"Come on, Grant. I've known you—what?—nine, ten years? You're a decent guy, and a good friend. You're no killer."

"I'm s'posed to think about it." Grant looked away. He drained the tall highball glass and set it down hard on the bar. "I could just hide in the weeds and shoot that mother—"

"Okay, look, give me your keys, Grant. You're not driving home tonight. I'll drop you off and we'll pick up your car in the morning. Come on, hand 'em over."

Grant hesitated a few seconds. He slid his keys slowly along the bar until they rested in front of Larry. Grant signaled to the bartender for their check while he fumbled to pull his wallet from his back pocket. Thank God it was a Saturday night. He'd be in no shape for work in the morning.

———∽∾∾⌾⌾∿∿———

It was a stormy Monday, the rain pouring down, flooding the parking lot at Saddleback Lanes. Inside it was warm and dry and Grant was having a pretty good night, playing up to his 170 average for a change. Gwen wasn't there and he was relieved. It was good to focus on his game, on helping his team gain a few points in the standings. The focus was about to shift dramatically.

The buzz went through the house like a Santa Ana zephyr. A guy on lanes 15 and 16 had a six-bagger—six strikes in a row. It was Ernie "The Wiz" Wizniewski, one of the best-known bowlers in the area, a left-hander with a silky smooth delivery and a ball that hit the pocket like a grenade. Just six more strikes and he'd have a perfect 300 game, his name permanently etched in the Saddleback records, and a big fat ring from the American Bowling Congress.

A shout went up from the crowd in back of 15 and 16: Wizniewski had made it seven in a row.

Grant knew what would happen if The Wiz kept this up. If he made it to nine in a row and stepped onto the approach for the tenth frame, needing three more strikes for a perfect game, the entire house would come to a complete stop. All thirty-two lanes, three hundred bowlers, the spectators and bar patrons, the arcade game players, and everyone else in the establishment, would pause in dead silence. Grant had seen it once before, a couple of years earlier. It was an awesome thing, the entire house paying silent respect to a solitary bowler, not wanting to disrupt his grand moment. He wondered what that pressure must be like, to stand on the approach with the only sound in the place coming from the clatter of the automatic pinsetters.

Another cheer from 15 and 16: The Wiz had made it eight in a row. The crowd was starting to swell near the center of the house, everyone anxious to be a witness.

A few minutes later came the loudest cheer yet: nine in a row. Now it began to quiet down, like someone slowly turning the volume knob to the left on a very large stereo.

Grant moved up to the gallery level to get a better view. He was straining to see over the crowd in front of him when he felt a hard blow to his left side.

"Geez...what the hell?" He jerked his head to the left.

Gwen was standing there, dripping wet from the rain, water running down her face, which was twisted into a pained grimace.

"You bastard! You lousy stinking bastard! You knew. You knew all along. And you lied right to my face. I thought you were my friend...*my friend*...and you used me, like a cheap little whore. You are a rotten...stinking...lying...asshole...and I hope you burn in hell!" She turned and ran for the door, disappearing into the crowd.

The murmurs went up all around Grant. *Hey, what the hell.*

Keep it down, man. Take it outside. Geez, there's a perfect game going here.

Larry moved through the crowd and put his arm around Grant's shoulder. "Well, there ya go, buddy. Now you can add 'User, Liar, and Asshole' to your resume." He laughed.

"Yeah. Right next to 'cuckold'."

"Come on, Grant. Let's go watch The Wiz make history."

"You go. I need a drink. A very stiff drink." Grant turned and headed for the bar, his mind whirling like a tornado. *Gwen knows...she knows. Sweet mother of God, what happens now?*

Down on lane 16, Ernie Wizniewski stepped onto the approach, bathed in silence. He set his feet carefully, adjusted his grip, and looked out on the lane to find his spot, just three strikes away from perfection.

Bright Angel

from *Monday Update*

A young man sat outside Trader Joe's, strumming his guitar, singing in a soft sweet voice. His guitar case lay open on the sidewalk, a few greenbacks and change resting on the red felt lining. And just like that, I was taken back forty years, back to 1976, and a guy named Will Mackinen.

I had moved into Sunrise Village, a new apartment complex in Citrus Heights, California, and immediately found myself part of a community. We were the first tenants to move in, everything bright and clean, the smell of fresh paint, new appliances and carpet. We began to gather, a dozen or more kindred souls, in the clubhouse, or around the swimming pool, to laugh and tell stories and toss back a few cold ones.

And then there was Will.

Will was a great guy and an instant friend. He always had a smile and a laugh, a hearty greeting. And he was seldom without his guitar. Will had a good voice; not great, mind you, but darn good. And he wrote his own songs, jotting down the lyrics on scraps of paper that he carried around in his guitar case. He didn't read or write music. The melodies were in his head, and it was remarkable how prolific he was, and how consistent. You'd think each performance of a song would be a little different. Not so with Will. He had a gift for musical memory.

As for style, I guess you'd call it Folk, or Soft Rock, or Folk

Rock. You get the picture. Will fit the genre perfectly. I'd say he stood five eight and weighed a buck fifty, his dark brown hair always carefully mussed, and I never saw him in anything but jeans and sandals. Throw in a great smile and a ready laugh and you had a guy who was easy to like.

After listening to Will a few times—gathered in the clubhouse, or on somebody's patio for a barbeque, or in one of the many lounges around the area where he booked weekend gigs—we had to ask the burning questions. *Will, why don't you cut a demo tape? Why don't you get those songs written down? Maybe you can sell them? Why aren't you on the radio, or TV?*

He was that good.

Will would just laugh and make a joke and sing another song. He said he might get his songs transcribed someday. But he didn't want to sell them. He only wanted Will Mackinen to sing his songs. That was frustrating for our little group. We were fans and we thought he should be a star.

Our community didn't stay long at Sunrise Village, just a little more than a year. People began to move on, for various reasons. Several couples got married; guys who were separated from their wives patched things up; others changed jobs and left the area.

I don't know what happened to Will, but he never made that big breakthrough and I never heard a Mackinen song on the radio. There were some pretty good ones, too. There was one about Will and a friend hitchhiking from Minneapolis to somewhere, and the friend asks, "Will, what happened to your women?" Here's the chorus:

> *Patsy is gone, Kathy isn't home*
> *Meredith is lost in Frisco*
> *Jill is still cold in the Minnesota snow*
> *Patricia loves a man who sings rock 'n roll*
> *Rock 'n roll...*

And then there was one called "New York City Woman."

Well, I'm a New York City woman
And you're a stranger in disguise
Hey mister can you spare a moment
You see my cigarette needs a light...

But the one Will had the most faith in, the song he was sure could be a hit, was called "Bright Angel." The chorus went like this:

She's a bright angel on a cool gray morning
First flower to bloom in the Spring
Some people are first with the warning
You're never sure just what she brings...

Forty years later and I still remember.

So, I listened to the guy outside Trader Joe's for a while, and then I dropped a couple of dollars in his case and wished him well. I wanted to ask if he knew a song called "Bright Angel," but I let it go.

He's good, but he's no Will Mackinen.

A Proper Salute

S heldon Klipstein was airborne, literally flying, like a soccer goalie diving to block a penalty kick. He had started up the stairs but changed his mind on the second step. He'd turned to his right, stumbled on a couple of magazines he'd dropped there, and now he was horizontal above the tile floor near the front door of his condo. He barely had time to say "Oh shit" before he landed—hard—on his right side. He took the brunt of the fall on his hip, his elbow, and the side of his head. The pain went through his body like a bolt of lightning, and the world faded to black.

———

He blinked his eyes and found himself lying on the cold tile, staring out toward the sliding glass door that led to his patio. He'd been unconscious, but for how long? He had no idea. Sheldon tried to move but the pain caused him to cry out. He settled his head back onto the tile, aware that a sticky liquid was pooled under his ear, and tried to assess the damage. It was bad.

"Oh Sheldon, you dumb shit. What have you done? The kids are going to kill you…if you haven't killed yourself already."

His three adult children had been after him for some time to sell his two-story condo and move into something all on one level. He'd resisted because he loved this place. It was his, the mortgage was small and affordable, the walls, tables, and counter tops adorned with family pictures and *tchotchkes* that meant the world to him. Besides, he was in great shape for a seventy-eight year old man and the stairs were never a problem. Until today.

God, what would Bernie say if she could see him now? His wife, Bernice, had been dead five years, and yet she was everywhere in the cozy three-bedroom condominium. The art she'd selected and framed adorned the walls, along with her photos of their grandchildren. Everywhere Sheldon looked, Bernie's touch remained. He knew exactly what her reaction would have been. First, make sure he was okay and the fall hadn't killed him. Second, she'd bring him a couple of Advil and a glass of water. Finally, she'd break up laughing until her sides hurt. That was Bernie. She couldn't help but laugh when someone stubbed a toe or banged a funny bone. But this was more than a stubbed toe.

Maybe if he could just sit up, his back against the front door, he could get his bearings and make a plan. Sheldon tried to move but the pain overwhelmed him.

"Rest a while...just rest...you bumbling *altacocker...*" His whisper trailed away. He shut his eyes tight against the pulsing pain.

———⁓⁓◦◦◦ᴓ◦◦⁓⁓———

Ivan Petrovich cruised slowly through the condo development, scanning for the telltale signs: newspapers left on walkways, mailboxes bulging with uncollected mail, business cards and real estate flyers piling up near front doors. All of these things spoke to him, saying, *I'm out of town, won't be back for a while, come on in and take my stuff.* How could people be so stupid? How hard could it be to stop the newspaper, have the mail held, or have a neighbor pick it up? Ah, but that would put Ivan out of business. Couldn't have that, now could we? He laughed.

His old white Chevy service van purred along smoothly. It looked like a piece of shit but he kept it tuned and the tires were good. He could drive it *from California to the New York Island* if he wanted to. He sang the old Woody Guthrie song to himself. *This land is your land / This land is my land...*

The magnetic signs on the sides of the van read "AAA Repair / Licensed Handyman" followed by a bogus phone number. The license plates were stolen, slapped on with magnets just before he turned into the neighborhood. The old Chevy had hauled away enough loot to keep Ivan in good Russian vodka, cigars, and lady friends. He loved Orange County.

He turned left into a section that contained a dozen or more units. "Hello! What have we here?" The unit at 195 Mulberry Place presented three uncollected newspapers. One appeared to be the Sunday edition, big and fat with ads, then two smaller deliveries, still in their orange plastic bags. Only three. Ivan's rule of thumb was four-or-more. But, business had been a little slow. The common parking area was empty, all the residents off to work on a Tuesday morning. He'd park in one of the spaces and check the mailbox for unit 195, then stroll up to the front door to see if there was an accumulation of cards and flyers. That would be his confirmation.

―――⁓ⱳ∘⌒ℯⱺ⊙⊙⊦ℯↄ∘ⱳⱳ―――

Mervyn Klipstein picked up his cell phone and speed-dialed his brother Leonard. It was nine fifteen on a Tuesday morning. His desk was overflowing with client files, but he had to talk to Lennie. Mervyn was worried.

Leonard answered promptly. "Hi, Merv. What's up? How's the family?"

"Hi, Lennie. It's all good. How's by you?"

"No complaints, Bro."

"Listen, Lennie, have you heard from Dad lately? I've been calling—his cell and his land line—but I get no answer and no call-back."

"Dad? Yeah, I saw him on Friday. He was over for *Shabbos* dinner."

Mervyn glanced at the calendar on his desk. "Yeah, but that was like, four days ago. You talk to him since?"

"No…no, I haven't." He paused. "Anybody over there we can call to check on him?"

"Not that I know of. It's probably nothing. You know he needs to upgrade that damn phone of his."

Lennie laughed. "Yeah, his iPhone was built by Steve Jobs himself."

"Right. Ya know, I think I'll call Myra, see if she's heard from him."

"Okay, Merv. Let me know what she says. I can run over there at lunch time if need be."

Mervyn ended the call and found his sister's work number in his contact list. Myra hadn't heard from their father either. They agreed it would be a good idea for Lennie to follow up. It was a twenty minute drive—allowing for traffic—from Lennie's office in Irvine to their father's condo in Aliso Viejo. Mervyn called his brother and left a message.

It was not unusual for the Klipstein clan to be out of touch for a few days, each of them busy with their own lives. Lennie had his law practice, Mervyn had his executive search firm, and Myra worked in a program at UCLA Extension that served students with intellectual disabilities. And then there was Sheldon with his passions for golf, baseball, jazz, and homegrown tomatoes. There just weren't enough hours in the day for the Klipsteins. All things considered, Mervyn knew they'd feel better when they heard Sheldon laughing, telling them to "Chill out, for God's sake. Why is everybody on *schpilkas*?"

Mervyn took a file from the top of the stack and went back to work.

Bernice was standing at the end of a long corridor, a bright light shining behind her. "Sheldon, why are you hollering? The neighbors can't hear you."

"Bernie, I've got to get help. I can't just lie here and...and die."

"They can't hear you, honey. They're at work, they're out to dinner, they're watching a movie. No one is listening, darling."

"I've got to try, Bernie. I've at least got to try."

"Come with me, honey. Hurry up now. I've always said you'll be late for your own funeral."

Sheldon's eyes snapped open with a rush of energy driven by fear. He mustered every ounce of strength that was left, pushed himself up into a sitting position, and moved back against the front door. The cost was horrendous. He tried shifting his weight to his left side to relieve the pain. It didn't help.

Through the sliding door across the room, he could see his favorite cup sitting on the patio table. He remembered now: he'd taken his morning coffee outside to enjoy the lovely August sunrise, came back in and started up the stairs to find his glasses. The plan was coffee and the Sunday *Orange County Register* on his beloved patio, surrounded by trees and shrubs and flowers. He remembered being annoyed that the *Register* delivery was running late.

Now he looked around, trying to take control of his situation. There was a small pool of blood on the floor to his right. He touched the right side of his head, just above his ear, and found where the blood came from. His pants were soaked. Somewhere along the line he'd lost the contents of his bladder. He could not stand up. It was useless to try, the pain too great. But he had to make a plan, to find a way out of this craziness. He felt a surge of emotion—anger, guilt, fear, then anger again. He was not going die like this. He would not give up. He shouted to the walls around him.

"As God is my witness...I'll dance at my grandchildren's weddings!"

Make a plan, Sheldon. Make a plan, damn it. He looked at the tile floor and tried to determine the distance from where he sat to the kitchen. His cordless phone rested in its charger up on the counter. If he could scoot himself into the kitchen, maybe he could find a way to knock the phone off the counter and into his lap—or somewhere within reach. How wide was each tile in the floor? *Think, dummy! Think!* Maybe eighteen inches. So every pair was three feet. That meant—*Damn it, Sheldon, concentrate!*—twelve feet, only twelve feet.

Movement out on the patio caught his eye. It was a man dressed in coveralls with a name patch on the breast, wearing a cap with a company logo. *Oh thank God!* Someone had come to rescue him. The man cupped his hands and peered in through the glass door. Sheldon motioned for him to come in, then closed his eyes and said a prayer of thanks.

"*Barukh attah Adonai, Eloheinu melech ha' olam...*"

Ivan stepped out of his van wearing coveralls and the cap with the "AAA Repair" logo. He carried a clipboard with a sheaf of official looking forms, a #2 pencil stuck behind his ear. He was the quintessential handyman come to answer a repair call. You had to be close to see that he was wearing latex gloves.

He checked the mailbox for unit 195. It was stuffed, at least two days of mail in there. No locks on the mailboxes here, just neatly labeled and out in the open. He grabbed the mail, picked up the newspapers from the walkway, and proceeded to the front door. Several cards lay on the doormat and a couple of door-hangers dangled from the knob. Ivan dropped the mail and the papers and tried the latch. The door was locked. *Whoa! What was that?* Was there a sound from inside? He listened for a few seconds. Nothing. Time to check the rear entrance.

Ivan walked down to the end of the street, turned right and

found the greenbelt that ran in back of 195, the second unit in. There was a gate that opened onto a patio. He took a quick look and saw a latch with a convenient pull cord at the top of the gate, then another deadbolt latch about midway down on the inside. The deadbolt was not engaged. Ivan pulled the cord, unlatched the gate and stepped onto the patio.

He approached the sliding glass door, cupped his hands around his eyes and looked in. *Well, well, well...lookee here!* Ivan smiled at the old man sitting with his back against the front door. The man waved for him to come in, then closed his eyes as his lips began to move. Ivan tried the sliding door. It was unlocked. He slid the door open and stepped in. He reached into the pocket of his coveralls and pulled out the Glock 19 pistol.

"Well, hello there! Are you having a bad day?" Ivan looked around quickly.

"Thank God you're here...help me...please. Call 911. I fell. I think I broke my hip—"

"Sure, no problem. Anyone else at home, Mr. ...?"

"Klipstein. Sheldon Klipstein. I'm alone...please help me...I'm in a lot of pain here...and I need water...please."

Ivan crossed the room and stood in front of Sheldon. "Glad to help, Shelley. Mind if I call you Shelley? Man, you are a hot mess! But first things first." He paused and looked around the room. "Nice. Very nice, Shelley. Like I said, first things first. I'm gonna have to take all your stuff, at least everything I can fit in my truck. Then I'll just hand you the phone and you can call 911 while I ride off into the sunset. How's that sound?"

"Take whatever...take it all...just give me the phone...and water...I'm begging you."

Ivan laughed. He turned and walked around, taking inventory. Flat screen TV, maybe sixty inch, looked new. Nice art, signed, numbered. Kitchen full of nice appliances. He opened the door to the garage. *Oooo, baby!* A late-model Lexus SUV. This would be a damn good haul! And he hadn't been upstairs yet. He was going to need help. Ivan whipped out his cell phone and called a friend. "Hey, Jaime. It's Ivan. Look, man, I've got a hot one here. How'd you like to make some easy money for a couple hours work? Let's say…three hundred. Deal? Okay, dude. I'm at 195 Mulberry Place in Aliso Viejo. Google it. There's a shopping center across Aliso Creek Road. Park your car there and get your ass over here. Make it quick."

This would be a piece of cake. They'd stage all the stuff in the garage, take out the old man's car, back the van in to load quickly, and be off to Freddie's warehouse up in Santa Ana. Freddie the Fence, famous for cash and carry. Ivan set his Glock on the kitchen counter and started up the stairs. The old man moaned as he passed.

"Hang in there, Shelley. This is gonna take a while."

———∿⌒⊙⌒⊙⌒⊙⌒∿———

"Sheldon, are you going to sit there all day?" Bernice walked past him and into the kitchen.

"Bernie, I've fallen and I can't get up."

"That's not funny, Sheldon. You shouldn't make fun of that commercial. It's a serious issue."

"But, Bernie, I am serious, honey. I've fallen—"

"Now stop it, Sheldon. How does brisket sound for dinner tonight? I have some left over. If we don't use it, I'll have to throw it out. You know how I hate to waste good food."

Why wasn't she listening? Sheldon gathered himself to yell at his wife, but the exertion caused him to move and the pain brought him back to reality. He opened his eyes to see two men hurrying around his home, their arms loaded with things he recognized: his laptop computer from the office upstairs, plus the inkjet printer; the stereo system and his collection of classic jazz CD's. The walls were bare. All of Bernie's fine art pieces, beautifully framed and hung with care, were gone. At least they wouldn't get Bernie's jewelry; that had gone to the kids or was locked away in a safe deposit box.

Sheldon felt violated, raped. He wanted to scream at these *goniffs*, these vermin, these assholes. But he couldn't do that. The one in the coveralls had promised to leave him the phone. He closed his eyes. He couldn't stand to watch any longer.

———————

Ivan's van was packed to the roof. They'd backed it into the garage and loaded it like professionals, tying down all the fragile items, covering the TV and the fine art with furniture pads. In the garage, they'd found top-of-the-line fishing tackle and a beautiful set of golf clubs. Going through the cabinets turned up an extensive collection of vinyl recordings. Add to that a half dozen dining room chairs, covered in what appeared to be fine-grain leather, and it made for an impressive load. Ivan was keeping a mental list and calculating what all of this would bring. He couldn't stop grinning.

"Wait till Freddie sees this. Show me the money, Freddie. SHOW ME THE MONEY!"

They were ready to move out now. Ivan took Jaime aside for last minute instructions.

"Okay, buddy. Listen up. You'll drive the van. I'll be behind you in the SUV. Take I-5 up to Santa Ana, no toll roads. Got it? Stay under the speed limit. We don't want any tickets, no attention from the Highway Patrol. You know where Freddie's warehouse is, right? Freddie knows we're coming. Remember I'll be right behind you." Ivan made like a pistol with his thumb and forefinger. He pointed at Jaime's forehead. "Don't mess up. Hear me? Do not mess up."

"Hey, homes, I got this. No worries." Jaime paused. "What are you gonna do with the old man?"

"What do you care?"

"He don't look good, Bro. He might not make it."

"So? One less witness. Look, just do your job. Got it?"

Ivan sent Jaime on his way and went back into the condo. He had one last item of business to attend to.

"Hey, Shelley. Wake up, man." He waited for the old man's eyes to open. "Time for me to go. Just wanted to say thanks for all the wonderful stuff. This was a nice place you had here."

"Oh God…please just give me the phone. I promise I won't dial 911 for five minutes—no, make it twenty minutes—after you're gone. I swear."

"Ah, Shelley, that's really sweet. But, there's been a change in plans."

"Oh no…please give me the phone."

"Can't do it, Shelley. I'm gonna exit through the garage, close it with the remote while I roll away in your Lexus. So I'm gonna leave you with the AMF Salute."

"The what?"

"The AMF Salute. It goes like this…" Ivan stepped back and stood at attention. He thrust both arms forward, the middle finger of each hand raised. "Adios, MotherFucker!"

He turned and headed for the door, laughing to himself, the most fun he'd had in a long while.

———⁓⦶⦶⦶⦶⦶⦶⁓———

Ivan rolled along Alicia Parkway, heading toward I-5. All he had to do now was cruise on up to Santa Ana and negotiate a good deal with Freddie. Man, would he love to show this haul to his dad. That old bastard always told him he'd never amount to anything, that he was too frickin' stupid to get out of his own way. What was his father's favorite saying? *Dumber than hammered shit, Ivan. You're dumber than hammered shit.* Ha! Wait till that old fart hears about this.

He came to a red light at the corner of Alicia and Moulton and sat there tapping his fingers to the satellite radio as Taylor Swift sang "Shake it Off." An Orange County Sheriff's patrol car pulled up on his left side. Ivan nodded and smiled at the officer. Instinct made him reach for the right hip pocket of his coveralls to touch his Glock. It was not there. He tried the left side. Not there either. *Goddamit!* It was all he could do to suppress a shout, a howl, a scream.

The light turned green. Ivan drove forward and turned into a residential area. He pulled to the curb and did a thorough search of his pockets and the interior of the vehicle. No pistol. *Sonofabitch!* He closed his eyes and retraced his steps from the time he'd entered the old man's home. *Shit!* He could see it clearly now, sitting on the counter in the kitchen. It was a damn good piece, that Glock. He loved that frickin' gun. No way was he going to leave it there for the cops to find. The condo was only ten minutes away. He dropped the Lexus into drive and flipped a U-turn, determined to retrieve his weapon.

———∿∾◦◦⊙⊙⊙◦◦∾∿———

Sheldon could pull himself along backwards about a foot at a time, each movement sending a shock of pain through his body. He would not quit. Now he was in the kitchen, reaching for the phone. It was set too far back. Another six feet across the floor was the drawer filled with odds and ends. There might be something in there—string, ribbon, something—he could throw around the phone and drag it off the counter. Sheldon looked up to the counter above the drawer. There sat the black form of a pistol and he saw that he could reach it. The final six feet across the floor were the worst. He rested his back against the cabinet, reached up to take the gun in his hands, and examined it carefully. And then he heard the garage door click and buzz as it rolled up.

The kitchen door opened and the man who wore the coveralls and the logo cap stuck his head in.

"Oh, Shelley, I'm ho-o-me!" The young man laughed at his own joke. "Well, look at you. All the way in here. Good for you, Shelley! Listen, I just need to get one thing and then I'll be gone. Okay?"

Sheldon raised the gun with his right hand and steadied it with his left. The sights wavered somewhere between Ivan's crotch and his chest. Sheldon surprised himself when he spoke.

"Shut up you little *schmuck!* You goddamn *putz!*"

"Whoa, Shelley, do you even know how to use one of those things? I don't think so—"

"Get the damn phone and give it to me, or I'll shoot you where you stand."

"Okay, okay, just be cool." Ivan crossed the room, sidestepping Sheldon's legs stretched across the floor.

"I don't want to shoot you. Just toss me the phone and get the hell out of here." The pistol grew heavier in Sheldon's hands.

Ivan reached for the phone with his right hand. "Okay, old man, here it is." He threw the handset—a hard backhand—at Sheldon's head. In the same motion, he dove for the gun.

Leonard turned onto Mulberry Place and found a parking space across from his father's condo. The garage door was open and he was relieved to see his dad's car parked inside. He started across the street and was stopped short by a POP POP POP sound and a sharp cry, like an animal in great pain. He ran into the garage and opened the door to the kitchen. There was his father, sitting on the tile floor, his back against a cabinet, a man in gray coveralls lying partially on top of him.

"Dad! What in the hell—"

"Get him off, Lennie. Get him off me—"

"What happened? Are you okay?"

"For God's sake, get him off. Call 911, call 911—"

Leonard continued to throw questions at his father—*are you okay, what happened, who is this man?*—as he grabbed Ivan by the ankles and dragged him back several feet. Leonard picked up the cordless handset where it had ricocheted off the cabinet and made the call to 911, his voice trembling as he asked for ambulance and police response.

Sheldon set the pistol on the floor. He stared at the top of Ivan's head and the smear of blood where Lennie had pulled him away, looking for movement, for signs of life. There were none.

Thou shalt not kill. Which commandment was that? Number five? Or was it six? That was between Sheldon and his God and he'd deal with it later. He made no gesture and he didn't say it out loud, but the salute was clear in his mind.

Adios, MotherFucker.

THE CONVERSATION

The waiter brought another glass of Cabernet and placed it on a fresh coaster. He removed the empty glass and the old coaster and smiled as Nick looked up from his book.

"There you go, Mr. Shane. Enjoy!"

"Thank you. I will." Nick returned the smile.

Nick was deep into *For Whom the Bell Tolls*, re-reading it for the umpteenth time, about to enter the chapter where Robert Jordan and Maria make love and the earth moves away. The wine was decent, Mr. Hemingway was great, and there was nowhere else Nick wanted to be. This was his favorite restaurant in Laguna Beach, a place where you could have a nice lunch and then linger for hours with a good book. The waiters all knew him, knew to keep his coffee cup or his wine glass full. Nick always tipped well and he never felt pressure to pay up and leave.

Chatter from the booth on the other side of the partition caught his attention. A man and woman ordered drinks, the waiter offered a cheery, "Very good, sir!" and hurried away. Though the couple spoke in normal voices, Nick could hear every word, as though they were sitting across from him. He glanced at the ceiling and decided it was some trick of acoustics. He tried to get back to reading but could not focus. He would listen quietly instead.

Him: "Pretty good movie, don't you think?"

Her: "I didn't care for it. I've never liked Ben Affleck."

Him: "Oh? Well, maybe we should have gone to the other one...what was it called?"

Her: "It doesn't matter. Just let it go."

Him: "Okay. So, what looks good on the menu?"

Her: "I'm not hungry."

Him: "What? Really? I thought you liked this place? That's why we're here—"

Her: "I said I'm not hungry. You can order. Don't let me stop you."

Him: "I'm not going to sit here and eat alone, for chrissake."

Her: "Then don't."

Nick heard the waiter's voice, back with their drinks. "There you are, for the lady...and for the gentleman. Now, are you ready to order?"

Her: "Nothing for me, thank you."

Him: "Okay...ah...just bring some chips and salsa. Thanks."

The waiter acknowledged and left the table. It was quiet for a few seconds.

Him: "So...what should we drink to?"

Her: "Is that necessary?"

Him: "How about...To us, and new beginnings."

The woman did not respond. Nick could picture the guy with his drink in hand, ready to touch glasses, and there he sat, hung out to dry.

Him: "Look...can we talk about this? What's the problem? What's wrong?"

Her: "Do we have to get into this now?"

Him: "Yes. Yes we do. You've been putting this off all week. It's never the right time to talk."

Her: "What do you want? What do expect from me?"

Him: "Look, you asked me to come home. You said you wanted to try again, to make our marriage work."

Her: "I can't just pretend that nothing has happened. You can't expect that."

Nick could hear the tension in both voices, the emotions beginning to boil. Now he was embarrassed for eavesdropping. This was none of his business. He took a big gulp of his wine, spilling a little on the tablecloth.

Her: "You've been out of the house for two years. Two years! I can't just jump back in like two years didn't happen."

Him: "Okay, okay. Calm down. I don't want to fight with you. But if this is how you feel, why ask me to come home?"

Her: "I'm going to the ladies room...and call the sitter, check on the kids."

Him: "Yeah, okay."

The man's voice trailed away. Nick looked around for his waiter, ready to pay his check and leave. Maybe he'd just take his check to the counter and pay there. He chugged the last of his wine as his waiter approached. "Ready to go, Mr. Shane? Here, I'll take that. Be right back with your change." Nick settled back in the booth and closed his eyes. He heard the man's voice, the conversation resumed.

Him: "Listen, can we start over here? Can we talk about it like adults?"

Her: "The kids are fine, in case you're wondering."

Him: "Of course they're fine. We've been gone for—what?—two hours?"

Her: "Finish your drink and let's leave."

Him: "Listen, Babe—"

Her: "I hate it when you call me that!"

Him: "Okay, sorry, Just let me finish."

Her: "Go on."

Him: "Maybe we could just start small. You know? A kiss when I leave for work, or when I come home at night. Maybe we could start by just holding hands?"

It was quiet for a moment. Nick looked around for his waiter. Geez, why wasn't he back with the change so he could leave a tip and get the hell out of here?

Her: "If you have to try that hard, maybe it just isn't worth it."

And there it was: a bomb in the middle of the chips and salsa. *If you have to try that hard, maybe it just isn't worth it.* Nick felt a pain in his chest; he'd heard it all before. He pictured the blood-red salsa all over the guy's face. The conversation next door was over. He heard the couple slide out of the booth and the click of high heels on the tile floor, moving away.

—⁂—

Nick handed his ticket to the valet outside the restaurant. The young man retrieved his keys and sprinted away toward the parking lot. He saw a woman and a man standing at the curb, waiting for their car. She was about five seven, long auburn hair that hung halfway to her waist, early thirties, attractive. The simple skirt and blouse she wore accented her figure. Nick didn't bother to look at the man. It would be like looking in a mirror.

The woman reached into her purse as their car arrived and removed a handkerchief. A ticket stub floated to the pavement. The man held the door for her as she settled into the late-model sedan.

Nick moved to the curb as the couple drove away. He leaned down to pick up the ticket stub, *Gone Girl* printed in bold type across one edge.

I should have said, 'Hey, buddy, come on over here, I'll buy you a drink. I'll buy you a whole bunch of drinks. All the goddamn drinks you want. And I'm gonna go see this damn movie, too. Ben Affleck is okay by me. Hell yes! I like Ben Affleck.'

Nick tried to calm himself as the attendant brought his car to the curb.

Moral Imperative

from *Lost Coast Review*

Have I got a story for you! You probably won't believe it but I swear it's all true. It's about two friends of mine, Adrian and Angela, a couple in their late twenties, and I'll bet it is the strangest story you've heard in a while. My name is Wilson—everybody calls me Will—and Adrian and I go back a long way, back to our grammar school days when he used to take care of me on the playground, make sure the bullies left me alone. You don't forget something like that. I mean basically he's a good guy. His concept of right and wrong gets skewed every now and then, but doesn't everybody's? Under pressure, extreme pressure, all of us will bend a little. Am I wrong?

But, I digress. Let me tell you the story and you can decide.

Adrian and Angela moved in together about a year ago. That is to say Adrian moved into Angela's apartment, a nice two-bedroom unit in a decent neighborhood. Angela mentioned the possibility one night in an intimate moment, if you know what I mean, and Adrian jumped at the offer, said yes so fast the poor girl didn't have time to change her mind. You see, Adrian is up to his eyeballs in student loans, can't afford the payments, and sees himself going down the drain. Angela has her own student loans to deal with, but at least she has a job. She's a registered nurse working at a local hospital.

Adrian's career choice was to go to film school at USC. He

wants to be the next Steven Spielberg and make blockbuster movies, but the best he could find coming out of school was a gig with an outfit that makes industrial training films. Hey, it's experience, right? So he takes the job on a contract and works for the company as an assistant director for about a year. And then—nothing. He's out of work. His bank account is draining rapidly. He's a few weeks from being flat broke. But then Angela threw him that lifeline, cut his expenses in half (or less) and kept a roof over his head. So he moved in and settled into the grind of trying to find work, trying to keep Angela happy, trying to keep his head above water.

You get the picture.

Angela is a sweet, sweet girl. Cute. Intelligent. Hard-working. And—here's the kicker—she loves to dance. I guess it's a way to decompress after a long week at the hospital, but Angela loves to go out to a hot club and dance her buns off. This is not Adrian's thing, but he goes along with it, mainly because after a couple of drinks and a night on the dance floor, Angela becomes a love-making tigress. Her passion knows no bounds. So Adrian dances till his feet ache and his ankles swell, with one eye on the clock. *Honey, think it's time to go? Maybe we should call it a night.*

Know what I mean?

So, one Saturday night they are in line outside this mega-popular club, waiting to get in. Angela is dressed to the nines in a clingy little dress that shows a lot of leg, and take my word for it, they are nice legs, especially when she slips on her Jimmy Choo knock-offs. How she can dance in those heels I'll never know. She must be related to Tina Turner.

But again, I digress.

Adrian is doing his best to keep up, wearing his Ralph Lauren jeans and a white linen shirt, untucked of course, unbuttoned at the collar, the sleeves rolled up a couple of turns. Off in the distance they can see the fireworks at Disneyland lighting up the night sky, the muffled boom boom boom arriving on a three-second delay.

The crowd waiting to get in is stretched out around the block. The security guys keep saying it will be a forty minute wait. A few people leave the club and few go in, but security sticks with the forty minute story. After a while, Angela has to pee. She holds it as long as she can but finally decides to head across the street to a service station with a food mart and use the bathroom. First she buys a couple of packs of gum to establish herself as a paying customer, then waits in a short line for the ladies' room. She is on her way back across the street when she sees Adrian heading toward her in a big hurry. Police cars are converging at the front of the club, their lights flashing, cops climbing out, wading into the crowd.

There was a fight, Adrian says. *Some girl got stomped. Come on, let's get out of here.*

On the way home, he tells Angela what he saw. Some people coming out of the club bumped into a girl waiting to go in. The girl yelled *WTF* or some such and before he knew what was happening, fists were flying, hair was being pulled, guys were jumping in to defend their women, and it was a full-blown brawl. The girl who got bumped wound up on the ground and she wasn't moving. At that point, Adrian decided to get out of there.

And that's the way the night ended. No dancing for Angela. No hot sex for Adrian. An all-around disappointing evening. Except for the part of the story Adrian wasn't telling.

———∿∽⌒☉⌒∽∿———

The next morning Adrian was up early and out of the apartment. He left a note for Angela saying he had to meet a guy about a possible job. He picked up the newspaper from the stoop on the way out and beat it down to his local Coffee Bean. He could not wait to check his iPhone and see the video he shot outside the club. And when he watched it all he could say was *Oh my God oh my God oh my God.* He had captured nearly all of the fight, including the girl throwing the first punch, including the ones who took turns stomping her head while she was down on the pavement, their faces clearly visible.

That's right: Oh my God!

He sat back in his chair and closed his eyes for a minute. Then he remembered the newspaper. He opened it and immediately saw the headline story about the incident at the club. The girl who was bumped, who took a swing at the woman who bumped her, who wound up down on the pavement getting stomped, was dead. They'd rushed her to the nearest trauma center but she never regained consciousness.

Adrian grabbed his phone and watched the video several more times. He picked up the paper and saw a companion column to the headline story, written by a well-known columnist—let's call him Scoop Smith—decrying the fact that nobody came to the aid of the girl as she was on the ground being kicked. And in spite of several people pulling out their camera phones to film the fight, no one wanted to come forward and help the police investigation.

There was a payphone just outside the coffee shop. Before Adrian headed for home, he called the switchboard at the newspaper and was transferred to Scoop Smith's extension. He left a voice mail message saying that he had important information about the club incident and that he would call again on Monday morning to discuss it. Adrian headed back to the apartment, hoping he could contain himself and actually wait until Monday.

———❦———

I know Angela pretty well and she is the epitome of a solid citizen, a straight shooter, the kind of person you want to be a nurse—your nurse. Sunday evening she curled up on the couch with Adrian to watch the news. The lead story was about the fight outside the club and the death of the young woman. Her name was Lia Nguyen. She was a recent graduate of a local college, a part-time model, and she wrote poetry as a hobby. On the TV screen flashed a still photo of the fight in progress, a girl with long brown hair on the ground, the group around her in obvious combat posture. At the edge of the crowd, a guy in a white shirt crouched down to get a better view, his camera phone held out in front of him.

Angela grabbed the remote and hit the pause button. *Oh my God, Adrian! Is that you? In the white shirt? That is you! What are you doing? You were standing there filming the whole thing? You didn't try to help her?*

Adrian did his best to deflect, but could see it was a lost cause. It was him and there was no way to deny it. He tried to explain that the guys in the fight were built like NFL linemen; at five nine and a buck seventy-five, there was no way he could help the girl. It wasn't long before Angela was demanding to see the video. He did some more foot dragging but finally got his phone and played it for her.

You have to take this to the police. This is evidence. You can't just sit here. A girl is dead... Angela let him have it with both barrels. She was disgusted to be sitting with him knowing now what he had done.

Adrian took a deep breath and made his case as forcefully as possible. *Look, Angela, this video is worth big money to these media whores. They pay for information like this. Look at the student loans you and I are struggling with. We could get enough from this to make a huge dent in that debt, if not pay it off altogether. We'd be stupid to just turn this over to the cops. Stupid!*

Adrian told me the debate raged on for more than an hour, loaded with tears and accusations, plus a discussion of morals and ethics in a morally and ethically ambiguous world. In the end, there was no way for Angela to be swayed. She issued an ultimatum: either he would turn the video over to the police or she would call them herself and turn him in. She agreed, after much pleading on Adrian's part, that he would do this by the time she came home from work on Monday.

Knowing Angela, I will never understand how Adrian bargained for that much time.

———·······———

I can tell you that Adrian is a hard-charger when he sets his mind to it. He was at it early Monday morning, as soon as Angela left for work. The first thing he did was upload the video to a bootleg copy of editing software on his iPad, a powerful package that he'd copied from the servers at the industrial film company where he'd been employed. The video was even more striking on his iPad screen. He could zoom and edit and frame the content and generally enhance the impact of what he had captured. He couldn't wait to show the results to Scoop Smith.

He found a payphone on the corner near a newsstand and called the newspaper. They patched him through to Smith's desk. Adrian made it short and to the point: he had clear footage of the attack on Lia Nguyen, footage that showed the faces of the people who stomped her to death. He wanted $120,000 for exclusive rights. Smith laughed and hemmed and hawed, but the bottom line was that he would have to see the video in order to determine if it was worth the asking price. They agreed to meet at a Starbucks in Towne Center. Adrian cautioned Smith to come alone; if there was any hint that he brought along a crew, or the police, the meeting would never happen.

———·······———

My friend Adrian is a clever guy, but he is no James Bond. He thought of a hundred ways that Scoop Smith could trip him up—bring a crew with telephoto lenses, alert the cops, wear a wire, and on and on. He decided to go through with the meeting anyway and showed up at the Starbucks forty minutes early. He plugged in his iPad and sat nursing a grande latte just like a half dozen other guys. At one point, he saw a discarded newspaper on a nearby table; on the front page was another article under Scoop Smith's byline. It seems that Lia lived in a neighborhood populated by senior citizens. She was friendly and chatty and did little favors for them from time to time. Her neighbors loved her and were grieving her loss.

Right about then, Smith walked through the door. Adrian recognized him from his picture in the newspaper. Smith ordered a tall Pike Place and found a seat. Adrian scanned the area to make sure good old Scoop came alone and wasn't communicating with anyone. Finally he picked up his iPad and approached Smith's table.

The introductions were brief. Adrian played the video footage a couple of times and Smith was duly impressed. Adrian had the goods, just as advertised. Then the two of them went into negotiation mode. Smith said, *Look, kid, we don't normally pay for information. Know what I mean? Checkbook journalism? We have our standards. Your video is impressive but I doubt that I can get that kind of money out of my editors. Besides, we're print media and you're peddling video.*

Adrian was prepared for this and he held firm. *Take it or leave it. Your parent company has TV stations, and there are a dozen other media outlets that I can reach out to. I thought of you first because of the column you wrote about the girl. I think a Pulitzer would look nice on your mantle, don't you?*

In the end, Smith agreed to take the deal back to his editors. Journalistic ethics be damned. Adrian would call him later that afternoon. And that was it. They went their separate ways. Adrian took a roundabout route back to the apartment, afraid he was being followed.

He may not be James Bond, but my pal Adrian is nobody's fool. Back at the apartment, he plugged external drives into his iPad and made a couple of copies of his video. He had a bulletproof idea for a place to hide the copies, just in case.

Angela called during her lunch break to see if Adrian had contacted the police. When he tried to sidestep and back-peddle, she hung up on him. In his mind he still had a few hours to make a deal with Smith; they had agreed that he would call at around 3:00 p.m. Adrian left the apartment and drove around looking for another payphone. It turns out they are not that easy to find, but he finally located one in the parking lot of a convenience store.

The call to Scoop Smith did not go well.

Look, kid, my editors won't go for it. At least not for the one-twenty large. I could maybe get you a few thousand, but that's about it. You know this is evidence in a murder investigation. You are looking at obstruction of justice or some shit like that. Your best bet is to call the police, give 'em what you've got.

So Adrian told him where he could stick his few thousand and hung up the phone. When he got back to the apartment, Angela had been there ahead of him. His suitcase and several trash bags stuffed with his things were sitting near the front door with a note.

Do not be here when I get home. Leave the key in the mailbox. I cannot be with a man who has no concept of morality.

Just like that it was over. Adrian went to the fridge and pulled out a beer. There were a few cold ones left and he decided to drink them all before he left. He would miss Angela, but hey, a guy's gotta do what a guy's gotta do. If she didn't want in on his debt reduction plan, that just meant more for him.

———— ◦◦◦◦◦◦ ————

Good old Adrian. Morally compromised, ethically challenged, whatever you want to call him. Even after three beers, my old pal still had the ability to think on his feet. He was about to head to the kitchen for another cold one when he heard car doors slam out on the street. He went to the window and saw two guys standing next to a gray Ford sedan, one of them checking his phone, the other leafing through a notepad. Dark rumpled suits, soft-soled shoes, aviator shades—obviously cops. How did they find him? Was it Angela? Scoop Smith? Or just good police work? To this day he doesn't know the answer.

Adrian immediately whipped out his cell phone and dialed 911. He hurried through the preliminaries with the dispatcher, even as the cops were walking up to the front door, and told the woman on the phone that he had just realized he had video footage of the fatal beating that took place Saturday night. He needed to speak to the police as soon as possible. She pointedly explained that this was *not* an emergency and that he should call the police directly. Adrian pretended that the connection was bad and hung up. When he answered the knock on the door and the detectives flashed their badges, he was ready.

Boy that was quick. I just got off the phone with 911. Come on in, I have something to show you.

———ᘛⁿᵒᵃᗉ✶ᗉᵒᵃⁿᘚ———

So, that's how Adrian came to live with me. Angela won't have anything to do with him, won't even consider taking him back; she's found someone else to take her dancing. Adrian sleeps on my couch and he's not bad as roommates go, picks up after himself, cleans up his own mess, and rinses out the sink after he shaves. In the meantime, he is hard at work on a screenplay. He is sure it can be a major motion picture, one of those based-on-a-true-story sensations. His concept is to eventually cut the real-life video footage into the film to give it that undeniable stamp of reality.

The cops took Adrian's phone and his iPad. They've never figured out that he has copies hidden away. They had their doubts about his story but the District Attorney hasn't charged him with obstruction. After all, he has that 911 call going for him.

We've had some long talks about what he's doing and whether

it is right or wrong. Of course, Adrian relates everything to a movie. In this case it's Clint Eastwood's *Unforgiven*, the scene at the end where William Munny blasts the saloon owner with a shotgun and Little Bill Dagget says, "You, sir, are a cowardly son of a bitch. You just shot an unarmed man." Munny says, "Well he should have armed himself..."

I asked Adrian to expand on that thought. Here he is in his own words:

"Will, my friend, let's face it. We live in a world where Wall Street CEO's can preside over a near-global meltdown of the financial system, throw our economy into deep recession, cause millions of people to lose their jobs, their homes, and their life savings. And what are the consequences? Those executives see their firms bailed out by the taxpayers because they are too big to fail. Then they pay themselves and their minions bonuses in the millions of dollars, and collectively spend hundreds of millions more to make sure that tough regulations are not voted into law. Lives are ruined, completely destroyed, and do any of these CEO's face prosecution or do jail time? Not a one. And what about students like me who took the easy money thrown at us by the banks—at eight percent interest or more? Now that interest rates are cut in half, can we refinance our loans and reduce the soul-sucking payments? Hell no! And why? Because those same Wall Street CEO's spend hundreds of millions to make sure legislation to help students never comes to a vote in Congress. Yes, Lia Nguyen is dead. But there is nothing I can do to bring her back. So, why shouldn't I capitalize on the video I shot? Why shouldn't I pay off my student loans with 'fuck you money'? Why just stand there and take the shotgun blast in the gut? No my dear, naïve Will, I choose to fight back."

All I can say to that is *Wow!* A masterpiece of rationalization. But then, Adrian could rationalize a heart attack. You probably noticed that last quote about *fuck you money* is also from a movie:

Matt Damon's character in *Promised Land*. With Adrian, it's all about movies.

Now here is the punchline: a production company wants to make Adrian's film. They are negotiating for an option on the screenplay and they're currently offering him $50,000. Not bad for openers. And let me tell you something: I've read the screenplay and it is damn good.

My friend Adrian has armed himself.

Note: This story is for Annie Kim Pham, killed in a fight outside The Crosby, a nightclub in Santa Ana, on January 18, 2014.

AFTERWORD

The most difficult skill in all of sport is to hit a round baseball with a round bat and hit it squarely. A great hitter in Major League Baseball, one who might wind up in the Hall of Fame, will carry a lifetime batting average at or above .300. Which is to say he will fail to hit safely in about seven out of ten at bats.

Consider two of the greatest players in the history of the game. Joe DiMaggio (Joltin' Joe, The Yankee Clipper) hit .325 in his thirteen-season career. Ted Williams (Teddy Ballgame, The Splendid Splinter) compiled a .344 average in nineteen seasons with the Red Sox.

So, what's the point?

I'm wondering: Does the metric for hitters apply to short story writers? For example, there are twenty-two stories in this volume. If you enjoyed just seven of them, it means I batted .318. I kind of like that statistic. It might not be Hall of Fame, but it ain't bad.

I hope you found *at least* seven tales here that touched you in some way and caused you to say, "Hmm…now there's a damn fine story."

That, Dear Reader, would make it all worthwhile.

ACKNOWLEDGMENTS

Two things are certain. First, a lot of effort went into this collection of stories—writing, critiquing, rewriting, editing, rewriting again and again. Second, there are some people who deserve a special note of thanks.

Chris Phipps is a former colleague from my days with Surewest Communications. Chris moved on to become an accomplished writer (check her out on Amazon.com) and a highly skilled editor. Also, a very tough critic. If these stories are worth reading, Chris is a major reason why.

Core members of the South Orange County Writing Critique Group reviewed most of these tales. I depend on the honest criticism and encouragement they provide.

Perhaps you noticed the number of stories with the acknowledgement "from *Monday Update.*" The editor/publisher, Harry Diavatis, took me under his wing in 2009 and has been publishing my work ever since. His fine weekly newsletter reaches more than 1,500 subscribers in all corners of the U.S. and as far away as Belize, Australia, and New Zealand. Thanks, Harry, for everything you do.

Finally, thank you to Barbara Spooner for working tirelessly to capture the cover photo. There were many candidates, but only one money shot.

Printed in the United States
By Bookmasters